A Chocolate Teapot

Raymond Austin

First Published in 2023 by Blossom Spring Publishing
A Chocolate Teapot Copyright © 2023 Raymond Austin
ISBN 978-1-7393514-2-7
E: admin@blossomspringpublishing.com
W: www.blossomspringpublishing.com

To Wendy, my wife, who always had patience and encouragement throughout a difficult time in this writer's life during the writing of Chocolate Teapot.

Also, my son Austin P. Austin helped me with the proofing for David my Blossom Spring editor again throughout a very difficult time. It would have never been completed without him and all at Blossom Spring Publishing.

Acknowledgement

For the help and input given to me by the seniors of the Haven retirement centre in Bedfordshire England.

Chapter One

Wendy had really pushed the boat out, lunch at the Ivy restaurant in London's theatreland round the corner from Covent Garden. Not an easy task to have pulled off considering she had made the reservation five weeks before! But it had been successful. The Ivy restaurant had been a firm fixture on London's dining and social scene since its foundation in 1917. In Wendy's younger days, she often dined at the Ivy. It was known in earlier years as the theatreland restaurant, mainly because it stayed open late, and you would always discover a star or member of the cast from one of the London shows dining after curtain down. Johanna, Wendy's daughter, had suffered the reminiscences of her mother's times at the Ivy over the years and could recount them word for word. Today the main thing was that Johanna and her granddaughter Rebecca had not been disappointed with their lunch adventure at the Ivy. The crowning of which for Johanna *and* Rebecca was to be sat two tables away from Ricky Gervais and Graham Norton who were lunching together.

* * *

The excitement of the lunch adventure had dwindled a little as mother, daughter, and granddaughter crossed Piccadilly Circus into Oxford Street. Wendy Knight was an attractive, slim, sixty-six-year-old woman, five feet nine, with blonde hair that showed some streaks of grey, which never bothered Wendy. '*Que sera sera*', was her motto. She wore a navy blue smart jacket and pants suit and was looking her best. They now walked arm-in-arm, daughter Johanna and granddaughter Rebecca. Johanna and Rebecca carried between them four plastic shopping bags, each displaying a store name, Harrods, Russell and Bromley, Fortnum and Mason, also Selfridges, they both wore blue jeans. Johanna was in her late thirties, with shoulder-length blonde hair, and as striking as her mother. Daughter Rebecca was fifteen, blonde, pretty, and wearing glasses. They crossed the noisy congested Oxford Street into Argyll Street. Animated, Wendy pointed along the street to the London Palladium, the marquee read '*A Chorus Line*'. As they arrived at the theatre Wendy skipped up the four steps leading to the box office and, to the amusement of onlookers, Johanna and Rebecca twirled around on the marble floor arms outstretched as Sinatra had done in the movie *On The Town*. Wendy who was in good voice sang the title, '*There's no business like show business*'. A family of three out of a dozen or so tourists watching Wendy gave brief applause which was taken up by the other onlookers with smiles and laughter. Wendy, very agile for her sixty-six years, tripped a light fantastic back down the steps to the pavement toward Johanna and Rebecca.

She slipped her arm around Rebecca's shoulder and hugged her close, Wendy looked back at the theatre. "The London Palladium. Rebecca, this is one of London's most famous theatres."

"Your grandma sang here," said Johanna proudly.

Rebecca nodded, all three stood and looked at the entrance in silence.

Wendy took her arm from around Rebecca's shoulder and looked at her. "I think our Rebecca is bored!"

"No, she's not," urged Johanna bumping hips with Rebecca, as at the same time she gave her the evil eye.

Rebecca took the hint, she took Grandma's arm. "No, Gran, I'm not."

Wendy laughed. "Come on, I want to show you one more thing." She moved them forward toward Great

Marlborough Street. The light-hearted three rounded the corner from Argyll Street arm-in-arm. Wendy pointed ahead of them to the large white lettering on the charcoal grey façade above the windows, it announced, '*The London Palladium*'. To the right of the windows, an arched entranceway with its oversized black gloss-painted door bore the legend '*Stage Door*'. She brought them to a halt, they stood and faced the door. Wendy was lost in thought and memories for a moment. *How many times had she walked through that door*?

Johanna brought her back to the now. "You're at home once again, Mum," she said with a smile.

"No, my darling," said Wendy, "this is the past. Home is where you, Dad and the family are."

Johanna slipped her arm around Rebecca's shoulder. "Your granny sang at a lot of theatres and clubs over the years, but mostly here at the Palladium, right, Mum?"

Rebecca moved to the stage door and reached out to touch it. "It's so shiny you can see your face in it," she said . . . "but it's gloomy."

Wendy laughed. "It's Monday, always dark on a Monday."

Rebecca frowned. "Dark?"

"Show biz saying, 'When a theatre is closed it's known as dark'," she enlightened Rebecca.

Rebecca nodded. "Because it's dark, makes sense."

Wendy nodded. "The rest of the week this doorway is hustle-bustle, actors and props go in and out, flowers being delivered. Honestly, it's a hive of activity. Your grandad would bring your mum here sometimes to the Wednesday matinees," said Wendy.

Johanna smiled as she remembered what a treat it had always been to come to London and see her mother on stage, especially here at the Palladium. Once she remembered going to Blackpool to see her mum as lead vocalist for a week at the Blackpool ballroom with the Ted Heath band. "Mum, we should stay another night and take Rebecca to the show tomorrow."

"Let's," hollered Rebecca.

Wendy groaned. "Not the same. There's no Ted Heath or Jack Parnell orchestras, with Wendy Knight as backup vocalist, anymore."

"No, but there's *Chorus Line*, da-da," sang Johanna.

Wendy stared at the stage door, saddened by the memories of yesteryear long gone.

Johanna looked at her mother. "Mum, you alright?"

"Yes . . . Memories, ghosts. I'd like a pound for every time I've been through that door," she said shaking off the gloom.

"You still miss it after all these years?" asked Johanna.

Wendy shrugged. "Yes and no."

The stage door opened and was held open by Henry Lynch, a grey-haired Irishman in his late sixties. He had a harmonica tucked in his shirt pocket. Two workmen carrying boxes forced Henry to step out into the street to let them pass. Wendy and Henry's eyes met briefly as he stepped back inside and closed the door. "Oh *my* . . . memories," murmured Wendy.

The stage door opened again, framing Henry. "*Wendy*?" said an apprehensive Henry.

Wendy smiled at Henry. "You just closed the door in my face, Henry Lynch."

Henry moved to her and she to him, and two old friends hugged. He stepped back and held her at arm's length. "God, woman, you haven't changed a bit."

Wendy laughed. "And you still know how to chat up a girl, Henry Lynch." They both laughed.

Wendy freed herself from his grip and turned to Johanna and Rebecca. "This is Henry Lynch, the legendary Stage Doorman of the London Palladium."

Henry beamed at his celebrity status.

"Henry, this is my daughter Johanna, and Rebecca, my granddaughter."

"Ladies it's a pleasure." He shook both their hands. "What are you doing here?" he asked.

"We came up for our twice-a-year shopping and theatre sprees," said Wendy.

"That's nice . . . Came up from where?"

"Ampthill in Bedfordshire," offered Rebecca, without a shred of her usual shyness.

"Indeed, country girls." He grinned.

"That's us," answered Wendy.

"You up for long?" he asked.

"No," replied Wendy, "we came up yesterday and went to see *Wicked* at the Apollo. Today was shopping and we are home tonight on the 8:10 train. This is our last stop before picking up our bags from the B & B. I wanted to show Rebecca where her granny used to work."

Henry turned to Rebecca. "Did you like *Wicked*?"

Rebecca nodded.

"Wendy, I tell you what, bring them in for a look-see," said Henry.

Wendy's face lit up. "Are you sure? We don't want you getting in trouble!"

"You're fine, it's quiet. Remember the routine. Two until five, take a break, go shop, or find a corner and get your head down, matinees an exception."

"I remember," said Wendy. She turned to Johanna and Rebecca. "You want to go see inside?"

"Yes." Rebecca tugged on her mother's arm.

Wendy raised an eyebrow and gave a nod. Henry stepped aside to let them pass. After he had closed the door, he led the way along the corridor stacked on one side with metal trunks and boxes. At the end of the corridor, they arrived at a flight of stairs leading down into darkness. Rebecca reached out and grabbed hold of her mother's hand. At the bottom, he turned on a light. There were two sets of double doors. Henry turned to Johanna. "Take yourself and Rebecca through there and sit yourselves down, in row A, seats A7 and 8. I want to give your mother a memory to take home."

Johanna nodded and led Rebecca through the double doors.

Wendy eyed Henry knowingly. He led her to the other double doors. "I know where this leads to," she said.

"It's changed a lot since your day, Wendy," he chuckled as he held one of the doors open for her.

As Wendy passed by him through the door, she tapped the harmonica in his shirt pocket. "I see you still have the harmonica."

"Yes indeed, you remembered," he said as they moved to the stairs that led to the fly-wings on stage left.

"Yes I do," she said. "You had a group of harmonica players – You were called The Harmonicas if I remember rightly?"

"You do have a good memory, come on." He led the way up the staircase.

* * *

In the auditorium, Johanna and Rebecca sat alone in row A, seats A7 and 8, their four shopping bags stacked on seat A9. Although dimly lit they could see that the stage was dressed and ready for the evening performance. Suddenly the footlights went on and startled them both.

Wendy and Henry stepped out onto the stage from the wings. Henry hovered back against the wings' curtains giving Wendy the stage. Slowly she walked out across the stage and looked out into the darkness beyond the glare of the footlights as she had done so many times in the past. The memories flooded back for her.

Johanna and Rebecca watched in silence. Wendy smiled as tears filled her eyes and ran down her cheeks. Johanna applauded from beyond the footlights. Emotions overcame Wendy, she brushed away a tear as she strained to look past the footlights. Rebecca added her applause to Johanna's. Wendy curtsied, as from the wings came the sound of music, it was from Henry's harmonica. He played the intro to 'Over The Rainbow' mellow and downtempo. Wendy looked at Henry leaning against the flat at the stage side wing. Her thoughts rushed back to Judy Garland's last television appearance, on this very stage, on January 19, 1969, she had filled in for an indisposed Lena Horne on the live *Sunday Night At The Palladium* show. Judy ended her performance as always with, 'Over The Rainbow'. Wendy, Henry and the other cast members had crowded into the wings for her performance. Wendy again looked at Henry, he winked at her and repeated the intro. Wendy took her cue and with trepidation sang, 'Over The Rainbow'.

Wendy's voice wavered but not Henry's harmonica.

Down beyond the lights Johanna and Rebecca were elated.

Wendy still nervous and unsure of her voice after all these years took a breath and continued the song.

Looking into the darkness beyond the lights things changed. Her voice became strong and in perfect pitch and key with Henry's harmonica.

Wendy's confidence was back and so was her voice.

After her performance, The London Palladium fell silent, but only for a moment.

Johanna, Rebecca and Henry applauded. Henry moved to Wendy and hugged her. "You've still got a voice, young Wendy Knight," he whispered in her ear.

Wendy stood back and looked past the footlights again, her eyes filled with tears. "Come on, you two, enough fun for one day," she called down to the girls.

"We're coming," shouted Rebecca, laughing as she followed Johanna through the exit doors. Wendy walked off stage with Henry.

"Darling Wendy, you've made my day. It's been a lovely thing seeing you after all these years," said Henry . . . He now had a tear in his eyes.

"I'm taking the girls to Langan's for an early dinner before the train, why don't you come along with us, my treat?" suggested Wendy.

"Oh, sweetheart, would that I could." He smiled. "I'm working on lates, I don't clock out till six in the morning. But I love you for the offer."

Wendy kissed him on the cheek. "Love you too, Henry . . . When are *you* going to put your feet up?"

Henry sighed. "Funny you should ask. I retire at the end of the month."

"Great," she said, "what are you going to do with yourself?"

"The one thing I'm *not* going to do is be put out to pasture, that's for sure," he said with a chuckle. "I'm going to keep busy. I lost the wife three years back, miss her like mad. No." He held up his harmonica. "I'm going to play this a lot more. There are four of us now that perform still, as The Four Harmonicas, we have a bit of a following."

Wendy looked hard at this man from her past and saw him in a new light.

"No, out to pasture would be bad for me," said Henry. "No way back from that, you get yourself stuck and you're finished . . . That would be retirement, to the grave."

Wendy laughed. "Good luck to you, Henry, and I'm

sorry for your loss," she said giving him a peck on the cheek.

"Thanks, Wendy." He smiled and they headed down the stairs and said their goodbyes on the threshold of the stage door of the Palladium.

Chapter Two

The 8:10 from St. Pancras to Flitwick hurtled through the early evening light. Johanna carried two polystyrene cups of coffee from the drink dispenser back in the centre carriage to Wendy and Rebecca upfront. Rebecca was curled up on the seat facing Wendy, her head resting on the plastic Harrods shopping bag; the other bags, plus the two wheely wheelies, were perched on the rack above. Johanna slid and dropped into the seat next to Wendy who sat staring out into the night as the dimly lit landscape flashed by. Johanna held the cup in front of her, to no response. "Mum, coffee," said Johanna.

Wendy turned to her, her train of thought gone. "Thanks, love." She took a sip of coffee. "Not bad, coming from a machine."

Johanna took a swallow of her coffee. "You're right not bad," agreed Johanna . . . "You were miles away, memory lane?"

"Something like that," said Wendy and smiled, "how'd you guess?"

"Henry – I could tell he brought back memories,"

she said.

Johanna nodded. "He can certainly play that mouth organ. I never knew one of those things could sound so good."

Wendy turned to her. "*Really?* You should have heard him and his buddies play. They played blues, jazz, you name it . . . He's retiring at the end of the month."

Johanna sipped her coffee. "That's sad."

Wendy turned to her. "What do you mean *sad*?" she snapped. "He's *still* going to work, maybe tour with his band."

Johanna shrank back in her seat. "*Okay*, I didn't mean sad, I meant . . ."

" . . . Sad," said Wendy. "You meant sad. God, you youngsters!"

"Mum, I'm hardly a youngster. I'm coming on forty."

"If I say you're a youngster, you're a youngster," said Wendy and drank more coffee. "This coffee is terrible."

Johanna shook her head and smiled as she let the silence hang.

Eventually, Wendy gave Johanna a sideways glance. "You think I'm sad?"

"*Mum*! *no*. It's a figure of speech, nothing more."

"Hmm . . . I'm sixty-six on Saturday and retired."

"Mum, it had to happen sometime! Old age comes to us all if we're lucky."

"*Lucky*! old age comes at a bad time, that's how lucky it is," mumbled Wendy.

Johanna frowned. "What do you mean, bad time?"

"I mean it's never a good time to get old," said Wendy, her hackles up.

"Since you stopped singing with the big bands you've been a vocal coach until the end of last year. *You're* the one who decided to retire."

Wendy took another drink of the coffee, which had become cold already. "I've retired twice!" she said. "Show business gave *me* up twenty years ago; what top artist or band needs a forty-year-old backup singer? So I took up teaching instead, and *now* I've retired from that!"

Johanna sighed. "Yours and Dad's choice."

"But I'm *not* sad," emphasised Wendy.

"Are you sad that you've loaned me your studio?" asked Johanna.

Wendy turned in her seat and faced her. "*No*, I am not and, don't you think it." Wendy turned back to the window and the night. There was silence but for the hum of the wheels on the track. Wendy broke the silence and mumbled, "*Sad*!"

"Will *you* stop it with the *sad*?" snapped Johanna exasperated.

Wendy turned back to her from the window. "Henry's not ready to lay down and die, he's going on the road with his band . . . I've retired, but I'm not *ready*."

"Mum!"

"I could still go on teaching," said Wendy irritably.

"No you can't," said Johanna. "That's what this is all about! You promised Dad you'd stop at sixty-five and you'd do all the things you've both been talking about and planning for years. *You* talked him out of it when you were sixty-five! He'll kill you if you do it again, now at sixty-six."

Wendy nodded and handed her her empty coffee cup. Johanna slid the cup into her empty one and placed them on the floor under the seat. She snuggled up close to her mother and rested her head on her shoulder. She closed her eyes. "Have a sleep, it's another twenty minutes . . . Mum? By the way, you were great on that stage. I'm so impressed and so was Rebecca. You should have been a soloist."

Wendy smiled. "I had my moments. Ted and Jack Parnell put me out front a few times, I was never quite good enough, but I could harmonise. You don't have to be a great singer to become a backup singer. There's life in the old lady yet. – A favour?"

Johanna leaned back and looked at her with suspicion. "*What*?" she asked.

"Don't tell your father about the stage bit, or the singing."

"Why?"

"Because."

"Okay, but you are going to have to talk your granddaughter into keeping that secret . . . and telling porkies for you, good luck with that."

They both looked across at the sleeping Rebecca, totally oblivious to all that had transpired.

Chapter Three

The village of Millbrook overlooked Ampthill Park on one side, and on the other side were twelve detached 1940s red brick two-story houses with pristine front gardens behind immaculate privet hedges. Wendy, in her robe, opened the front door of number 2 with mail in her hand. She stepped outside onto the welcome mat and took a deep breath of the morning air.

"Morning, Wendy," came Phil's voice from the other side of the hedge.

Wendy stepped out onto the garden path that looked to the gated gap in the hedge, this led to the garden of number 4, and their neighbours, Phil and Dot Roberts. Phil was a good-looking man in his mid-sixties.

Wendy smiled. "How's Dot's finger?" she asked.

Phil closed the gap. "Still broken," he chuckled.

"Funny," said Wendy as she realised the stupidity of her question.

Phil was dressed casually and carried a bowling bag. He opened the gate and sidled up to her. "It's inconvenient, but she's managing. Have a good weekend in London?"

Wendy walked back to the front door followed by Phil. "Wonderful." She reached the door and called into the house. "Ray, Phil's here with his toys." She smiled at Phil. "He wants to know if you can go out and play."

From inside Ray hollered back, "Can I?"

Wendy motioned to Phil. "Come on, coffee's brewed."

* * *

Wendy and Phil entered the large open-planned country kitchen. Its windows overlooked the garden and small patio. The coffee in the percolator bubbled away. Wendy put the mail on the table. "You want a Danish?"

"I'm good, Dot made me breakfast, coffee's fine," answered Phil.

"Coming up," said Wendy. She hummed to herself as she moved to the percolator and then to Phil with a mug in her hand and poured him coffee, she knew he took it black.

"You're happy?" said Phil reacting to her happily humming.

"I am . . . Always happy when I go to London, brings back memories."

Phil nodded. "Your years singing with the bands?"

"They were that good." Wendy poured herself coffee. "London always brings back the good old days."

"A trip down memory lane," Phil prompted.

Wendy sat facing him. "You know, Phil because we're seniors a lot of folks think we're all washed up . . . On the heap, out to pasture. Just about as useful as a chocolate teapot . . . Well, we are *not*."

Phil laughed. "Chocolate teapot! Where did that come from?"

Wendy raised an eyebrow. "You know what I mean," she said with a hint of frustration. "What would happen if you were to put a chocolate teapot to work with hot water?"

Phil shrugged. "It would go gooey, melt and collapse."

Wendy nodded. "Right, that's the way society thinks of folk of our age. *Don't* give us too much to do we are past it, we'll collapse on the job. Wrap us up in cotton wool and mothballs and put us in the bottom drawer."

"While I don't disagree with you," agreed Phil, "you've certainly got yourself a bee in your bonnet now you're a senior."

"*Phil*, it's nothing to do with being a senior – It's *not* being wanted as a senior, we're put on the shelf!"

Wendy went to the Aga and with an oven-gloved hand slid the tray of Danish from the oven, placing them on the cooling tray.

"Can you keep a secret?" she asked.

Phil crossed his heart.

Wendy sat back down, elbows on the table, and faced him. "I'm going to put together an ensemble of senior ladies and teach them to sing. We are *not* going to be put out to pasture."

"Sing what, and where?" he asked.

"Songs. Where? Anywhere and wherever anyone wants to be entertained."

Phil stared back across the table at her – "Why?"

"Because I'm not ready to become a chocolate teapot. And I'm sure I have lots of senior friends who'd feel the same way."

"By senior you mean?" asked Phil.

"Sixty, and older if they want. None younger than fifty."

Phil laughed. "Isn't that age discrimination in reverse?"

"I guess it is. That's ironic," laughed Wendy.

"Ironic it is," said Phil conjuring with the possibilities.

"But *is* it possible?"

"Why wouldn't it be?" Wendy shot back at him.

"Women of that age, *your* age, have obstacles, most obviously, husbands!" he said nodding.

Wendy nodded back. "Yes, there will be obstacles, including mine." She looked up at the ceiling, indicating their bedroom above and her husband Ray upstairs.

"No you're good, Ray would be your biggest supporter."

Wendy shook her head. "Ray's a wonderful husband, but he's looking forward to my retirement. That's why it has to be a secret. He can't have any idea of my plan, yet. I can count on you?"

Phil chuckled. "I don't want him mad at me."

"That will never happen. And for the record, I don't want *anyone* to know," she emphasised. "Not even the seniors I'm thinking of."

"Daughter Johanna?" he asked

"*No*, especially Johanna. She can't keep a secret!"

"Where are you going to rehearse this ensemble? Do you still own the studio?"

"The building yes. Johanna runs her arts and craft studio there. Can't have classes there. Plus she'll blab."

Ray Knight, Wendy's husband, dressed for bowling, sixty-five and carrying a touch too much weight, entered the kitchen holding his empty coffee mug. He went to the sink and rinsed his coffee mug. "How goes it, Phil, ready to get beaten again?"

"No. I've had enough, I'm going to win today," answered Phil.

Ray dried his hands. "We'll see. Ready?"

Phil finished his coffee. "Thanks for the coffee, Wendy."

Wendy nodded with a smile. "You're welcome."

Ray kissed Wendy. "See you later. I'll get a sandwich for lunch."

"Okay, love," she said and whispered to Ray, "Let Phil win for once."

Ray smiled. "No," he whispered back at her. Ray and Phil left. Wendy refilled her coffee and slid the stool over next to the phone. She sat and picked up the phone and punched in a number.

She got a connection. "Arlene, Wendy . . . Yes thanks, great time . . . I would have but we got back late, listen, do you think you could get the girls together for a lunch? It's important, I want to talk something over with you all

. . . Right, see you." Wendy put down the phone and took a sip of coffee and smiled artfully as was her way when she was up to something like mischief.

Chapter Four

Wendy drove into the parking lot of the Chequers pub in her black and white Smart Car and parked. She took her faux Gucci bag from the passenger seat and climbed out of the little car. Wendy always dressed well and was known for it, but today she looked very classy in the new navy blue blazer she had brought on their London shopping spree. She had added a pink shirt, jeans, and suede loafers, and jauntily swung her faux Gucci bag over her shoulder.

Two workmen carried decorating materials from the side door of the Chequers to their truck. The older of the two watched Wendy set the alarm on her Smart Car. "What's that, *half* a car!" he chuckled.

Wendy headed for the pub. "No," she called back over her shoulder, "as anyone with *half* a brain can see."

The younger workman laughed and called out to her, "Good one, lady."

As Wendy went through the pub door she waved thanks for the compliment.

* * *

Music played softly over the speaker system in the Chequers. There were a dozen or so lunchtime customers seated around the spacious bar enjoying bar food and drinks. Kelly, a young, pretty African Caribbean barmaid, waved to Wendy from behind the bar as she entered, Wendy waved back. She spotted Arlene and her friends at their usual table by the window, all had their customary drinks in front of them. Arlene was sixty-seven, petite with grey hair. Her clothes, although smart and colourful, were mumsy. Jan, sat to her right, sixty-three, lanky, all legs and arms and as thin as a beanpole. On the other side of her, was Emily, seventy, of average weight and height. Emily always appeared to be nervous and was a giggler, she giggled at most things, funny or not. Wendy joined them and sat in the usual seat that had been kept for her.

Before Wendy had a chance to utter a word, "Did you have fun?" asked Arlene excited for news of her excursion.

"I did! You won't believe what happened to me," said Wendy as she cosied up next to Arlene.

Kelly called Wendy from the bar, "*G & T, Wendy?*"

Wendy gave her a big smile. "*Please.*"

Emily giggled with anticipation at Wendy's news of

what had happened to her on the London trip. "Wendy do tell us," she begged.

"Did Rebecca enjoy *Wicked*?" asked Jan.

"Yes, so did Johanna, it was fabulous. I've told you about the restaurants, the Ivy and Langan's before. *Well*, I took them to the Ivy for lunch and Langan's for early dinner before the ride home."

"We thought you'd take them someplace like that," said Emily impressed. "I'd love to go there. Did you see any stars or anyone you knew?"

Wendy nodded, again and again. "Graham Norton and Ricky Gervais."

"Did you know them?" asked Arlene.

"No, my time at the Ivy was before they were born."

Kelly arrived with her G & T. Wendy took her faux Gucci bag from her shoulder and took out her faux Gucci purse and handed Kelly two twenty-pound notes. "Fill us up all round, Kelly, and one for yourself."

Kelly took the money and headed back to the bar for the refills. Wendy took a sip of her Gin and Tonic and looked across at Jan. "After the Ivy lunch I took them to see the London Palladium."

Emily let out a gasp, followed by a giggle.

Wendy rested her hand on Jan's and looked around the table at her friends. "You are not going to believe what happened."

Chapter Five

All but two of the bowling lanes were in use *and* by seniors, mostly men. Ray bowled and took down ten pins. He clapped his hands together and spread them wide. "*Yeah*, way to go." He moved back to Phil at the bench, sat and picked up his beer.

"Phil, how long have you known me?" asked Ray.

Phil got to his feet. "Since the day you and I signed on at Taylor's Heat and Air."

Ray sipped his beer. "that would be thirty years."

Phil picked up his ball. "Must be. We were the best heating engineers Taylor's ever had."

"True," said Ray.

Phil bowled, and he took down seven pins. He let out a grunt. "A wee touch to the right and I'd have had it."

Ray stood and laughed. "In your dreams." He moved to play. "You know, Wendy has had a working life as long as I have!" He bowled, taking a nine. "Darn it . . . *Near one*. A touch of hook and I'd have had the lot."

"In your dreams," mimicked Phil.

Ray moved back to the bench and sat next to Phil.

"We're supposed to be going places now we're retired –
Nothing fancy, but away. We've planned to pack up the
car and take some runs over to Europe. Spend some time
in Spain, and France. Just get away for maybe three to
four months of the year."

Phil nodded. "So why aren't you?" he asked, feeling
uncomfortable knowing Wendy's plans for her retirement
and the promise he'd made to keep her secret.

Ray shook his head. "I bring it up once a month but it
sort of gets swept under the carpet."

Phil smiled. "Maybe you should bring it up once a
week rather than once a month!"

"*Maybe*," Ray mumbled to himself. "Maybe. You'd
think she'd be only too pleased to get away for a bit. She
used to go all over the place way back. God, she travelled
the world for close to fifty years, twelve with the Heath
band."

"Your Wendy had a heck of a life," pondered Phil.
"She must have loved her work to stick at it all those
years."

Ray thought about what Phil had said. "Yes, she did.
Ten years ago she could have packed it in. *No*, we bought
the studio and she set up the voice school. That was

supposed to close on her sixty-fifth birthday and away we'd go on our travels . . . She's still hanging on to it!"

Phil eyed Ray. "She loves teaching the young ones, you know that." Phil picked up his ball and lined up on the pins.

Ray nodded. "Given the chance, she'll be teaching the old age pensioners to sing next," Ray joked.

Phil saw the funny side and lost his concentration. The ball left his hand and drifted into the gully, a dead ball.

"You're not paying attention," Ray chuckled.

'*Oh I am*,' Phil said to himself. "Ray, you can never tell with Wendy what she's going to be up to next."

Ray gave a nod. "I've become used to that over the years," he agreed.

Chapter Six

Wendy startled them all as she thumped the table. "*I . . . sang . . . on . . . stage!*" she announced.

Recovering from the shock of the table being thumped, all were ready to hear more.

"It was exciting to be back there in front of the footlights, looking out over the auditorium," she said.

"But it *was* empty?" ventured Arlene.

"*Yes* . . . but for Johanna and Rebecca. Arlene, that's not the point, I was back on a stage singing."

Emily giggled. "All your memories must have come flooding back," she said, genuinely happy for Wendy. Wendy had shared her memories of her showbiz career, over and over, with her friends and they never seemed to tire of the anecdotes.

"You're right, Emily," said Wendy as she looked around the trio. "But what's more to the point? I'm understanding what keeps nagging and nibbling away at my brain."

Jan took a swig of her drink. "What are you talking about? "Wendy took a mouthful of her G&T and looked from one to the other. "We're *not* finished at sixty-five or our seventies . . . We still have lots of life in front of us."

"This revelation after singing at the Palladium?" laughed Jan.

"No . . . *Yes*. Not on the stage necessarily, we could sing if we wanted," urged Wendy.

"Hold on . . . Is this the royal we? Are you including us?" asked Jan.

"I sing in the shower, that's about it, and not too well at that," admitted Arlene.

Wendy eyed Arlene. "You don't know that. All of you, you've never had me take you under my wing, and you've never been to my classes."

Jan frowned and looked at the others. "You want us to become a group, like the Three Tenors?"

Wendy laughed. "Tenors we would not be, but a group yes. Not just three of us, we could be bigger."

"I used to sing in the choir at St. Andrew's in Ampthill," Emily giggled.

"You're serious," said Jan shaking her head.

"Yes," answered Wendy enthusiastically.

Arlene fixed Wendy with a stare. "I hear wheels turning in your head, Wendy Knight. What about Ray and your retirement . . . Your world travel plans? You told him sixty-five, it's already stretched to sixty-six."

Wendy frowned. "I can retire next year, sixty-seven is just around the corner."

Emily giggled. "You're bad, Wendy, but it sounds fun."

"Please, Emily, don't encourage her," said Jan.

"Emily, I bet you can still sing. Listen, you three, would you say you're past your sell-by date?"

"Hell no, I'm still dating," answered Jan with pride.

All eyes went to Jan. Emily giggled, then stared wide-eyed at Jan as did the others.

"What?" asked a self-conscious Jan, taking in their reaction.

"I never knew you were dating," said Wendy wide-eyed.

The others agreed in unison.

"Well, *I am* . . . I do . . . not at the moment but . . ." Jan nodded a yes.

Arlene forced her attention away from dating back to Wendy and her singing. "Let's get this right. You want to form a singing group and perform someplace or the other?"

Wendy nodded. "Right, I'm not ready to be put out to pasture as yet."

"Wendy you've lost it," said Jan.

"No, I haven't." Wendy folded her arms and leaned forward on the table. "Seniors, sixty-five and up."

"Crazy," murmured Arlene.

Wendy's brow wrinkled. "Yeah, crazy like a fox." She turned to Jan. "What do you mean you're dating?"

Both Arlene and Emily leaned forward, elbows on the table, determined not to miss a word.

Jan did something she had not done in a long time, *she blushed.*

Chapter Seven

The weather forecast at the end of the six o'clock news popped up on the eighteen-inch television, tucked into the corner of the kitchen countertop. Ray picked up the remote at the side of his wine glass and turned the television off. They sat at the table, empty plates before them. Wendy nursed a glass of red wine. "Great meal, you know lamb is my favourite, with minty sauce," said Ray.

"Of course, I know," answered Wendy, "it's always been your favourite!"

The phone rang, and Ray reached across to the countertop and picked up the cordless phone. "Hello, *hello* . . . Don't ask me, I'm not the weather bureau." He hung up and placed the phone on the table.

"Who was that?" asked Wendy.

"Wrong number. Some guy asking if the coast was clear."

Wendy threw her napkin at him. "That joke is older than I am, besides all of my lovers know to hang up if a man answers. Who was it?"

"Robocall, electronic voice selling insurance." He took a sip of wine. "That joke can't be older than you, we never had a weather forecast sixty-six years ago," Ray chuckled.

"You are hopeless," said Wendy, "but that's one reason I love you."

"Ditto," said Ray. "You haven't said much about London. Did the girls enjoy it?"

"Yes . . . Sorry, I thought I'd told you, they had fun. We did all the sights."

"They liked *Wicked*?" he asked.

"Yes, we all did. God, Ray, there is so much talent in that show."

Ray sat silent and studied her. She knew full well she hadn't told him about the London trip.

Wendy watched the wine as she swirled it around in her glass, knowing Ray was watching her. "What!" she said eventually.

"What, what?" was his answer.

"You're looking at me."

"I'm allowed." He finished his wine" . . .You miss it don't you?"

Wendy looked at this kind gentle loving man she had

spent the best part of her life with, she did not want to hurt him. "Yes, we all miss what was good . . . but it's gone and I'm looking at the new."

Again silence hung, as Ray smiled and gazed into *his* empty glass. Then the penny dropped. "New! What new?"

Wendy was on the spot. "Life's new every day."

Ray studied her thoughtfully. *Life's new every day.* "Did you show them the Palladium?"

She was tempted for a moment to tell him everything about what happened at the Palladium, but . . . "Yes." To the visit, but no details. She finished her wine.

"Good." He watched her, and she smiled. "Looking forward to Saturday night?"

She dropped the smile and looked puzzled. "Saturday?"

"The senior citizens dance," he said.

"Oh boy," said Wendy, "I'd forgotten, old age catching up with me."

Ray frowned. "How can you forget? You virtually took it over this year, with Louise in and out of chemo."

"I know, I know . . . My head's been someplace else. I was also worried about Louise. She's now in remission and I don't want to steal her night."

"No one including her is gonna think that. Besides which, it's your birthday as well . . . *That's it*, I forgot! You don't like birthdays, especially your own."

"I do too," she said, knowing he'd hit the nail on the head, "but only every five years. I'm tired, I think I'll leave the washing up till the morning, early night?" She stood and smiled at him.

Ray gave her an even bigger smile. "Sounds good to me." He stood and offered her his hand. A touch coyly, she took his hand and they headed for the door, the stairs, the landing, the bedroom, and the *bed*.

Chapter Eight

Wendy had done the rounds of Waitrose Supermarket and wheeled her full cart across the parking lot to the Smart Car. She opened the boot and loaded the week's shopping.

"There's more room in that little car of yours than one thinks."

Wendy turned, and Phil and his wife Dot stood behind her; they too had a cartload of groceries. Dot was in her sixties, a handsome woman. Wendy immediately spotted Dot's splinted finger.

"Hi," said Wendy, "everyone's always surprised to see how much room there is in my little Smarty Pants."

Dot chuckled. "Smarty Pants, that's cute."

"How's the finger?" Wendy asked.

"Ruddy inconvenient," answered Dot holding up her splinted finger.

"More to the point, how's the planning going for your senior ensemble of songs? Phil told me of your chocolate teapot analogy."

Wendy turned to Phil, then Dot, she frowned. "Phil,

it's supposed to be a secret, remember? Wet your finger, cross your heart hope to die stuff. Like only yesterday!"

Phil felt embarrassed. "But not from Dot," he said as a way of an excuse, "she can keep a secret."

"Better than you I hope," said Wendy, "you're as bad as Johanna."

Dot came to Phil's rescue. "It won't go any further, Wendy, I promise. But do tell, what's the plan?"

Wendy closed the boot and leaned back against Smarty Pants. "Well, it's like this . . . Mind you I haven't got a plan worked out yet, but . . ."

Chapter Nine

Wendy and the clan regularly met at the Health Club in Woburn twice weekly, today was no exception. Wendy, Arlene, Jan, Emily, and Kay, a sixty-five-year-old. Kay died her hair jet black and always wore too much make-up, but she was a lot of fun. All the ladies were in a row on the treadmills and walked at a brisk pace to the piped music, Wendy in the centre.

Kay questioned Wendy between breaths, "You took the family to the Palladium . . . sang on the stage and took a trip down memory lane . . . and *now* you want us to form a singing group?"

"In a word, *yes*," answered Wendy.

"We'd need our heads examined," sniffed Kay.

Emily interrupted, "Wendy, I told you I sang in the choir . . . but it was a while ago, I've forgotten most of what I knew," she said somewhat breathlessly.

"Emily," said Wendy, "the keyword is *most*. It'll come back. It's like riding a bike, you never forget."

"But you can fall off," quipped Arlene with apprehension.

"I never learned to ride a bike," giggled Emily.

"I'll teach you," offered Jan.

"Great, so you're with me?" said Wendy.

"Hold on," Jan snapped. "I only said I'd teach her to ride a bike."

"Right," Wendy snapped back, "and I'll get her singing voice back, same difference."

"Same difference!" said Arlene and stopped her treadmill. "What does that mean, the same difference? It's got nothing to do with it."

Wendy stepped off her treadmill and grabbed a towel. She stood in front of the others; all shut down their machines and focused on her.

"Now you listen to me," said Wendy, addressing her troops. "We're written off when we get into our sixties. I don't want to be written off. As far as I'm concerned I still have lots to do with my life. So, if any of you feel the same, not wanting to be left at the roadside, now's the time to step up."

The ladies exchanged looks, and then Arlene came to the fore. "First let's hear what your plan is?"

"Right, conference, the Chequers. Drinks on me," said Wendy to her troops.

Chapter Ten

The gang: Wendy, Arlene, Jan, Emily and Kay sat at their window table in the Chequers, drinks at hand as Wendy had promised. Wendy had their attention. "I'd like to rekindle our singing ambitions, with say seven including me."

"I didn't know I had singing ambitions!" murmured Kay.

Jan frowned. "I don't know that I ever had the ambition to sing!"

"Ditto," agreed Arlene.

Kay looked at Wendy. "It's going to be all seniors?"

"Do you think we can do it?" giggled Emily with a sparkle in her eyes.

Wendy nodded. "Yes if you four are on board. My only other problem is getting two more to sign up."

"You're going to have your work cut out!" warned Jan.

Emily leaned forward. "I know Mrs Meng from the Chinese Takeaway will join. She's always singing at the top of her voice. Her daughter is in your class, remember?"

"I'm impressed, Emily," said Wendy. "That's a good thought, we have a start. Will you talk to Mrs Meng? Remember, at the moment it's a secret, especially from Ray, that is at the moment," she emphasised.

Jan raised an eyebrow. "You're going to lie to him?"

Wendy looked at Jan indignant. "*No*."

"Yes!" said Jan. "You haven't told him anything about the Palladium, about you getting up on stage and singing?"

"It's not a lie . . . I've just not mentioned it yet," answered Wendy, knowing she was in between a rock and a hard place.

Jan was like a dog with a bone, she would not let go. "It's a porky, period."

Wendy avoided eye contact and swirled her wine around the glass. "For the moment it's a little secret, that's all . . . not an outright lie."

"What's a porky?" asked Emily puzzled.

Jan looked at her. "A porky is a lie. It's Cockney rhyming slang, porky, pork pie, pork pie lie."

Emily frowned. "Doesn't make sense, it's easier to say lie . . . Pork pie is nothing to do with it, and besides, it's longer."

"Emily, just pretend I never said it, okay?"

Emily shrugged.

Arlene thought about it. "It's a big little secret . . . you're going to start a seniors' singing group?"

Wendy nodded. "Yes, and again it's not a lie as such. It's a secret. Now can we stop the inquisition? Ray will be alright with me keeping a little secret for a while."

They exchanged looks, then looked back at Wendy, unconvinced.

"I still say it's a lie," insisted Jan, "but forever onwards."

"What's the next move?" asked Emily.

"It's Wednesday," said Wendy. "Let's all think about it, and Monday we'll see where we're at."

"Are we all going to be at the seniors' dinner and dance on Saturday?" asked Jan.

They all affirmed the seniors' dance Saturday night.

"Good we may even have some names by then," said Wendy with enthusiasm.

"Right,' said Jan, "don't hold hopes up high. Even if we dimwits have agreed we still need two more dimwits to make it work."

"I'm sure we can count on Mrs Meng," giggled Emily forever confident.

Wendy held out her glass initiating a toast. "To Mrs Meng."

All agreed in one voice, "Mrs Meng."

Chapter Eleven

Ampthill Seniors Centre had been beautifully decorated by the women of the seniors' committee and the caterers. Chairs and tables dressed in pink linen and glittering tableware lined the left and right walls. Two tables, again with pink table linen, stood against the end wall adjacent to the entrance, laid out with welcoming wine, canapés, and paper napkins. Thirty or so couples with their families in tow hovered. An additional dozen couples danced to vocalist Johnny Royal's rendition of 'Moon River', backed by six instrumentalists of The Johnny Royal Dance Band.

* * *

Wendy's clan, minus Wendy and Ray, arrived with their husbands all in the same age range. Arlene and Ken, Jan with her new friend from online dating, Frank, Emily and Brian, Kay and Gary, Dot and Phil. The ladies wore cocktail dresses and the men black ties. There were lots of hellos, shaking of hands, and kisses on the cheek as they moved toward their custom fifteen-person table number one. Eventually, they all found their way to their seats. There were five empty chairs left at the table.

Ken pointed to the empty chairs. "She's forgotten her own birthday!"

Phil laughed. "No, I talked with Ray this afternoon, they'll be here. But remember, Wendy only recognises birthdays once every five years."

They all laughed.

'Moon River' ended. Johnny Royal had a quick word with the pianist and went back to the microphone. "Ladies and Gentlemen. It's time to take your sweetheart in your arms and show them what the years have meant." Royal turned to the band and counted them into the intro for 'Time after time'. Most got to their feet including all the ladies and husbands of table number one.

Johnny Royal turned back to the microphone and sang. As the song continued, Wendy, Ray, Johanna and Kevan, Johanna's husband arrived.

Kevan a good-looking man in his mid-forties brought up the rear with his daughter Rebecca. They paused in the doorway, caught in the romantic moment of the song and the dancing couples.

Ray took Wendy by the arm and whirled her onto the dance floor and into his arms. Johanna, Kevan and

Rebecca smiled as they edge along the dance floor. Johanna nodded and waved to friends as they weaved their way to their table.

Wendy and Ray were lost in the lyrics as they danced, reminded of their good fortune and deep love.

Wendy and Ray danced close. Ray whispered, "Now are you glad we came?"

Wendy whispered back, "Yes thank you."

"For what?" asked Ray.

"Marrying me." She kissed him on the cheek.

He hugged her close, spinning her around in his arms as the song ended and applause echoed around the room. Royal and the band took a bow as the dancers returned to their seats or mingled. Wendy and Ray joined the others.

Arlene surreptitiously manoeuvred her way through the crowd toward Louise Bellwood a striking woman, in her late sixties. Louise wore a silk scarf tied close to her head, she had lost her hair during her bouts of chemo. Louise and her husband Paul, a portly man in his sixties, were talking to Johnny Royal at the foot of the stage. Arlene approached and said something to both of them. Royal gave a nod. A moment of conversation took place, and then Arlene headed back to the others, her excursion unnoticed. As she sat, from the stage came a fanfare and a drum roll.

Johnny Royal took the microphone. "Ladies and Gentlemen . . . Ladies and Gentlemen please." The room quietened, and all eyes went to the stage and Royal. He continued, "May I have your attention please for your entertainment secretary Louise Bellwood!" Applause erupted, Johnny Royal stepped to the side and took Louise's hand, and brought her to centre stage in front of the microphone. Louise carried two sheets of paper with her notes on them. Royal stepped back giving her the floor. Again, applause erupted – Louise smiled and held up her hand, and the room quietened. She cleared her throat. "Ladies and Gentlemen. If I could have a moment. I'd like to thank you for your support tonight." She looked down and read from her notes, "To date, including tonight, we have raised £8,390 for the new heating and air-conditioning equipment for the old wing." Again applause filled the room. "Thanks to you all for being so generous and giving . . . Thank you." The room fell silent. "As you know, Ray Knight and Phil Roberts are coming out of retirement and donating their time to install the new equipment for the centre." Louise tucked her notes under her arm and began the applause. Guests from all parts of the room waved at Ray and Phil, who reluctantly stood and waved back. Louise held up her hand and the room quietened. "I know you want to get on with the dancing, but let me take a moment more of your time. As you all know I have had to take a backseat over the last year for obvious reasons," she said patting her head, producing some restrained laughter and an attempt at spasmodic applause. Louise continued, "Many of you came to my help, thank you all. But now, on a lighter note, I think you all know I've had good news, I am in remission." This brought on cheers, whistles, and a standing ovation. This time Louise let the applause subside in its own time looking around at the faces that had comforted her in thought, word, and deed over the past months. *'She would always remember this and cherish the joy on their faces as she stood there, tears welling. She bathed in their happiness.'* She took a tissue from a sleeve and wiped away her tears, as she mouthed thank you, over and over. At the same time, she quieted the guests, raising her hands above her head. The prolonged applause waned and was replaced by the sound of chairs being moved back in position around the tables and people sitting. Louise had everyone's attention once more. "I'm sure you all know there's a friend that took the workload off my shoulder." She pointed at table number one and Wendy. "Wendy Knight." Again applause all around, people stood and continued to applaud. Louise moved across the dancefloor to Wendy and mid the applause brought her reluctantly back to the stage and in front of the microphone. Louise signalled for quiet and the applause died. Louise slipped her arm around Wendy's waist and shouted into the microphone, "And it's her birthday." Applause, whoops, shouts and laughter filled the room. Johnny Royal motioned the band, they struck up Happy Birthday. Everybody burst into song as a cake with candles was brought to the stage by Arlene, followed by everyone from Wendy's table. Wendy's tears flowed.

Chapter Twelve

The congregation milled around chatting and moving to their cars after the Sunday service at St. Andrews. Johanna, Kevan, and Rebecca exited the church followed by Ray, Wendy, Phil and Dot. Dot spotted Mrs Meng and moved over to talk with her. Lian Meng, a short agile Chinese woman of sixty was a Christian and had worshipped at St. Andrews since she and her family had moved to Ampthill from Luton fifteen years ago. It had been a surprise to the locals in Ampthill, who expected her and her family to be Buddhists or something like that.

Ray and Phil talked to other churchgoers. Arlene and Emily were chatting in the background.

Rebecca turned to Wendy, a touch too loud. "Gran, why is it a secret about the Palladium?"

Wendy spun Rebecca around, hiding her from Ray. She looked at Johanna. "Did your father hear?"

Johanna looked past Wendy to her dad. "No, I don't think so."

Rebecca whispered, "Gran . . . Why?"

Wendy looked at Johanna and Kevan.

Kevan moved closer to Wendy and said softly, "Wendy, whatever you're up to *again*, we don't want to get in the middle of it."

Wendy slipped her arm around Rebecca and hugged her. "Rebecca love, it's a secret for now, but in time your grandpa will know." Wendy looked at Kevan. "There, that's the truth."

Kevan glanced at Johanna and raised his eyebrows. Johanna looked back at him. "Don't look at me!"

"*Mrs Wendy . . . Mrs Wendy.*" Called Mrs Meng.

They turned to see Mrs Meng as she hurried toward them, followed by Dot and the others.

Mrs Meng came to a stop face-to-face with Wendy. "Mrs Wendy I sing your class?" she said in her strong Chinees accent.

Dot arrived and looked at Wendy sheepishly. Mrs Meng continued for all to hear, "I sing, Mrs Dot, tell me, I sing."

Arlene and Emily overheard Mrs Meng's joyful outcry, as did Ray and Phil. All inched up to Wendy. Wendy's eyebrows raised as she looked at Dot. "And what about the word *secret* don't we understand?"

Dot forced a smile which caused her nose to wrinkle.

"You agreed we were going to ask her," she said and smiled at Mrs Meng with a nod. "Mrs Meng," she added with another nod.

Arlene leaned closer to Wendy on seeing Ray closing in on them. She whispered to Wendy, "We did that. We said we were going to ask her." Ray was almost upon them. Still, in a whisper, Arlene added, "No lies, remember?"

Ray entered the group. "What are you ladies up to?" All eyes went to Wendy. "Ray, you remember Mrs Meng, she was in my voice classes," said Wendy, not ready for this discussion at this juncture.

Ray remembered and smiled at Mrs Meng. "Yes, hello again." Ray shook her hand, but felt uneasy . . . Something was amiss, all eyes were on him!

"I sing Mrs Wendy?" said Mrs Meng.

"Yes you did, and very good you were," Wendy said patting Mrs Meng on the shoulder. She looked at her audience who eagerly awaited her response. *How was she going to get out of this one?* Wendy broke the silence, "Excuse us a moment, student and teacher stuff," she said looking daggers at Phil and Dot. "You understand," she said sweetly growling. Wendy slipped her arm around

Mrs Meng and took her aside, leaving all but Arlene and Emily somewhat confused.

Chapter Thirteen

The six ladies: Wendy, Arlene, Dot, Emily, Jan and Kay formed a procession through the car park and headed to the Chequers entrance.

Kay announced en route that she hated Mondays. "Why are we meeting today? I have so much to do on a Monday!"

Wendy went right back at her, "Because we said we'd meet on Monday."

Jan chimed in, "Because we said we'd meet on Monday. If you didn't want to meet on a Monday you should have said."

"I think it's exciting," said Emily with a giggle.

"Emily, you'd find paint drying exciting," growled Dot.

From the far corner of the parking lot, Mrs Meng hurried toward them, calling out, "Ni hao", Chinese for *hello there*. "Ni hao, Mrs Wendy, ni hao."

Wendy turned in her stride and looked at Dot.

"I promise, ha! Who else did you tell, Dot?" said Wendy.

"Only Ray," said Dot.

Wendy stopped dead in her tracks and turned on Dot.

Dot threw her hands up in defence. "Joke, it's a joke . . . besides, anyway we need Mrs Meng."

The others agreed as Wendy turned and waved a welcome to Mrs Meng. "I know that, that's why I told her we were meeting today," lied Wendy.

Mrs Meng, all smiles, caught up to them as they entered the pub.

* * *

The Chequers was quite busy, music played as Kelly cleared plates and glasses from the window table, and the ladies chose their seats around the now set table. They greeted Kelly, who smiled and took their drink orders. Arlene started in on Wendy as soon as her bottom hit the chair. "Wendy, you are *sure* you're serious about all this?"

Dot nodded. "The last we knew you were going to retire this year for sure."

"*I know*. But a person can change her mind," Wendy justified.

"You should exchange yours, it's not working too well," laughed Jan.

Wendy pulled a face, *haha*. "I've had the desire to have a senior women's singing group on the back burner for a long time."

"Looks like you've turned up the heat . . . and I'm finding that a little spooky," murmured Kay.

"Spooky," repeated Emily.

"I aim to make people sit up and take notice of us and we can do it by singing."

"I sing lots since Mrs Wendy tell me how," said Mrs Meng with a big contagious smile. they all smiled back at her.

Wendy looked from one smiling face to another, ending on Mrs Meng. "Mrs Meng, there is no need to call me Mrs Wendy, just Wendy is good."

"That good. I no Mrs Meng, I Lian, mean *the graceful swallow*."

Without hesitation, Wendy introduced everyone by name to Lian, which seemed silly as they had known and been getting their Chinese Takeaway from her for years. But Wendy went ahead anyway and pointed at each in turn. "Arlene, Dot, Emily, Jan, and Kay."

Kelly arrived with their drinks, minus Lian's. She looked around the table. "One short. Sorry, Lian, you want your Guinness?"

"Yes, Guinness, Kelly."

The gang exchanged looks and pleasantries until Lian's Guinness arrived. Wendy put up a toast. "All agree with my plan?"

There was a little trepidation but, in the end, they raised their glasses and drank. All echoed the one refrain from Wendy's toast, "*Agreeing.*"

"*Maybe,*" Jan added as an afterthought.

"Jen, don't whinge," snapped Wendy. Her arms went out, embracing all around the table. "Picture us, senior ladies, singing as a group, dressed to the nines in swanky costumes."

Arlene shook her head. "Is *this* a horror story?"

Emily baffled asked, "Why would we need swanky costumes?"

"Maybe not swanky, that's the wrong word. You know what I mean, dressed up in matching outfits, the audience loves a show."

Jan reacted, "*Hello* hello, audience?" she exclaimed. "Audience! Did I miss something? Where did we get an audience from?"

"We'll get an audience," Wendy groaned and shook

her head. "The whole point is that people sit up and take notice. They stop looking at us as being old biddies who are past it and have been put out to pasture – If people are going to take notice of us, they have to see us."

The gang of six listened without comment, *knowing* full well the feeling that all and sundry from time to time had been looked at and treated as if they should be wrapped in cotton wool and mollycoddled. They looked at each other in consideration.

Again Wendy did her all-embracing arms gesture to the ladies. "For audience read people. We're not going to be looking for fame and fortune, and our names on the marquee. Listen, you all know how useful a chocolate teapot is. I want us to show the world we are not on the heap at our age . . . also I think we can have a good time and prove to them, *like husbands* . . . they are wrong about us." Her sales pitch took a little time to sink in, but when it did there was a glimmer of understanding of what she was all about. "There is one thing I will promise you, I *will* make songbirds out of you . . . we will sing. We'll do shows, personal appearances, and so on."

"Where?" asked Dot.

Emily jumped in, "Senior citizens' centres," she said

excitedly. "We are always asking people to come and talk, play the piano . . . Anything we can get."

"See, already we'd have a built-in audience." Wendy smiled.

"We're senior citizens," added Kay.

"Listen, it's a start . . . who knows what's around the corner?" Wendy encouraged.

Arlene took a swig of her drink. "I have a question. Since you handed over the studio to Johanna and she is operating it as such, where would *we* hold classes?"

Wendy beamed. "Rehearsal. You're using the royal *we* already, that's a good sign."

The senior citizens looked at each other. Jan shook her head. "I don't know how it happened . . . but I guess we are hooked."

Lian smiled and clapped her hands. "We sing, yes?"

There were smiles and nods all around, then sips, and gulps of their drinks.

"One small thing?" said Jan.

All eyes landed on Jan.

"We now need members."

"And to find out which of us can sing," said Kay.

Lian became very animated. "I know this song." Lian

indicated the pub's in-house speaker sat high on the wall, and Ella Fitzgerald was singing 'Let Yourself Go'.

Lian continued, "I sing with Ella, Wendy."

With that, Lian sprang to her feet, swaying to the music of Ella Fitzgerald's 'Let Yourself Go' and sang along with Ella; amazingly without a trace of her Chinese accent, *and* she was good. The gang were gobsmacked, including other customers around the bar. Lian sang and moved to the beat. Wendy gave the others a thumbs up. Then called out to Kelly, "Kelly, turn up the music."

Kelly hit the volume, and that did it . . . Wendy was on her feet next to Lian and they accompanied Ella to the last note. A big round of applause went up from all the customers of the Chequers. Kay got to her feet and hugged Lian.

Arlene laughed. "Well, I never, you were both . . . both so, so good."

Lian Meng smiled. "I no forget, Wendy."

"No, you don't, Lian, that was good," praised Wendy.

Kay and Lian sat back in their window seat, as did Wendy. Wendy looked at the gang in turn.

"What did I tell you? We're going to have ourselves an ensemble after all."

Arlene, Jan, Kay, Dot, and Emily looked at each other.

Arlene looked down in the mouth. "After hearing you two I'm going to need a refresher course and fast!"

"Put me down for the beginners class," said Jan.

"Ditto," agreed Kay.

Emily giggled. "Double ditto."

Emily turned to Dot, who looked at the group. Dot shook her head. "Not me . . . I'm your seamstress, stagehand, whatever, a singer I am *not*."

Everyone laughed as Wendy eyed her seamstress. "You're on, bless you, Dot." Wendy beamed.

"Dot first job, give us your thoughts on seven outfits. Something simple, but needs to be elegant."

Emily chirped in, "Something befitting our age."

"Ruffles maybe?" suggested Kay thoughtfully.

Wendy clapped her hands. "There you go, we're on our way. Right, we need one more to make the team. But please, ladies, keep my Ray out of the loop."

Arlene eyed Wendy. "You still haven't told him?"

"I'm going to," answered Wendy, not very convincingly.

"Wendy why seven," asked Emily," . . . why not six, four, or eight?"

"Seven is a good number and sounds good for an acapella group," explained Wendy. "I've been thinking acapella as I don't see us affording a band *or* musicians at this stage."

Jan smiled. "What a shame, I was hoping for a full orchestra."

Everyone laughed.

Chapter Fourteen

Ray and Phil cleared the fallen leaves from their postage-stamp front lawns: Phil by hand, Ray with his electric blower. Both reacted to Wendy's Smart Car as it pulled into the driveway, Wendy climbed out and waved to them both as she headed for the side door into the kitchen.

* * *

The faint hum from Ray's blower outside increased as the back door opened and Arlene popped her head around the door. Wendy spun around hiding something behind her.

"Ha-ha . . . caught you, what are you hiding?" asked Arlene as she stepped into the kitchen and closed the door reducing Ray's blower back to a hum.

Wendy breathed a sigh of relief. "I thought you were Ray!" Relieved, from behind her back she revealed a stack of sheet music and a folder. "I'd marked this lot to give to the Salvation Army, but we are going to need them now," she said indicating the music.

"Wendy! You're gonna have to tell him what you're up to," said Arlene. "It's going to be tears before bedtime, mark my words."

Wendy put the sheet music in the folder and placed it under the vegetable rack tray. She crossed to the dresser, opened the centre drawer and brought out a bunch of travel magazines and brochures. She dropped them on the table and looked at Arlene. "Vacation magazines – He picks a new one up every week."

Arlene looked at the magazines. "If we're going through with this you're going to have to tell him. You've turned us all into conspirators."

Wendy nodded. "I will . . . I'll tell him, it's unfair on you all." Wendy gathered up the magazines and put them back in the drawer. She turned to Arlene with a frown. "What are you doing here?"

"What am I doing here? God my brain is getting addled with all this subterfuge . . . See what you're doing to me! – Yes, Emily had an idea, her husband Brian has his carpentry workshop over behind Park Place and a barn out back he doesn't use."

Wendy beamed. "Would he let us use it for rehearsals?"

Arlene nodded. "Emily asked and he said yes."

"Oh yes," squealed Wendy, "and he'll not tell on us."

"*Wendy*, you have to tell Ray!"

"I'm going to . . . I am," she said, ashamed, knowing she had no idea how she was going to do it. She had made a promise about retirement before and broke her promise. "That's great about the barn," she said changing the subject. She was conscious that the hum of the blower had stopped. "It's all falling into place," she continued. "Hey, would you like a sandwich and a glass of wine?" Again changing the subject.

"Best idea you've had so far, please," said Arlene.

"What will it be, ham, cheese, or tuna?"

"Yes," said Arlene.

"Yes? What do you mean, yes?"

"You asked me, ham, cheese, or tuna?" repeated Arlene and sat at the kitchen table.

Wendy frowned. "That's right . . . so what will you have?"

"Ham, cheese, and tuna," Arlene answered confused.

Wendy turned to the refrigerator mumbling, "You're hopeless."

The back door opened and Ray strolled in. "Ladies."

"I'm making sandwiches said Wendy, would you like one, sweetheart?"

Ray sat next to Arlene. "Sounds great."

Wendy made Ray the same offer, "Ham, cheese, or tuna?"

"All of the above," said Ray and gave Arlene a big smile.

Arlene looked at Wendy, raised her eyebrows and shrugged. "See, all of the above!"

"Just seen Ian from the garage," said Ray.

Wendy started work on the sandwiches. "Yeah."

"He says you and Lian Meng did a cabaret turn in the Rose and Crown today," said Ray. "A whole group of you ladies whooping it up. What was that all about?" he asked.

Wendy sneaked a look at Arlene who was hiding a smile behind clenched teeth. "Just clowning around," laughed Wendy.

Ray nodded. "He said you were very good."

Wendy's eye met with Arlene's again, as at that moment the back door opened and Johanna stepped in.

"Hi all . . . Mum, I hear you and Lian Meng were giving a concert at the Rose and Crown!"

Wendy looked daggers at them all. "*Yes,* It's going to be on the BBC news at six and in the morning papers."

Chapter Fifteen

Ray had let Wendy sleep in, he thought. He was at the point of putting the finishing touches to a breakfast tray he had prepared for her when she came into the kitchen in her pink robe.

"Sweetheart." Wendy sighed. "I was going to bring *you* breakfast in bed! How long have you been up?"

"Not long. You were spark out when I got up," answered Ray.

Wendy moved to him and hugged him around the middle and kissed him on the cheek. "You're a darling," she said endearingly. "I'll go back to bed." She faked heading for the door.

"No, you don't . . . No point, you're up! Sit yourself down."

Wendy pulled out a chair from the table and sat. "Sorry, darling, it was a nice thought though."

"I thought so," he said as he placed the tray in front of her. He then poured coffee for them both and sat facing her. "What's the modus operandi for today?"

Wendy buttered her toast and reached for the

marmalade. "I'm going to put in a little time at the centre."

"Right . . . is Louise managing okay?"

"Seems to be. I thought I'd see if there's anything I can do, just help out a few times a week while she gets back on her feet."

Ray frowned. "A few times a week!"

Wendy's brain was racing, she had put her foot in it! *Trying to make an excuse for why she was going to be out of the house more than usual.* "Well maybe now and again, help where I can."

Ray nodded as he stole a slice of her buttered toast. "Right – we need to make some plans soon about our trip." He took a bite of the stolen toast. "I thought Spain could be fun for starters?"

Wendy also took a large bite of the newly buttered toast. Playing on the fact so she could not answer with her mouth full, she nodded. Moments passed, her mouth now empty she needed to say something! "Right, what you up to today?" was all she could come up with!

"Car service," said Ray.

"Not Smarty Pants?"

Ray chuckled. "No, your other car, the one you let me

drive – It doesn't have to be Spain, we could do France this year!" he pushed.

Wendy knew she was in trouble; Ray was not going to let it go. "Spain . . ." There was a knock at the back door . . . saved by the knock she took a breath.

"That'll be Phil, he's going to run me back from the garage." Ray opened the door to Phil.

"I could have brought you back," she said.

"Morning all," said Phil.

"Morning," said Wendy. "You want coffee?"

He looked at Ray. "Do we?"

"Sure, I've got to shave, take ten," said Ray.

Ray got up, kissed Wendy on the head and made his way up to the bathroom. Phil took his chair as Wendy reached for a cup and poured him coffee.

Phil leaned across the table closer to her and whispered, "Have you told him yet?"

She placed the coffee in front of him.

Still, in a whisper, Phil prompted, "Your plans . . . Does he know?"

"Hush," snapped Wendy softly.

"I am hushed."

"No, not just yet," she had to admit.

Phil grinned. "I see . . ."

" . . . No, you don't," she said, still in a whisper. "And yes, I am going to tell him. I want to show him ladies of our age still have a lot going for us. We just need a little practice, then I'll show him and tell him at the same time."

"I see . . . I think you'll find he knows that already," he said doubtfully. Then on a brighter note, "I heard that you and Lian Meng don't need much practice."

Wendy spread her hands in the air. "God! everyone in England knows me and Lian Meng."

"No," said Phil with a smile. "Only in Ampthill."

Wendy gave in, she had to see the funny side of it, and she smiled.

"Wendy – tell Ray. You're digging a deep hole for yourself and it's going to be difficult to climb out."

"I know Phil *and* I know my Ray let me do it my way."

He gave her a puppy-dog look, shrugged and took a sip of his coffee.

Chapter Sixteen

Emily's husband Brian only used the barn that was behind his workshop to store wood and remnants of broken furniture from over the years. Brian and Emily stood in front of some broken chairs and other pieces of furniture stacked high. Wendy, Arlene and Dot stood in the open doorway with Jan and Kay looking over their shoulders, all with a look of apprehension on their faces at what hopefully was going to be their rehearsal space. As the ladies looked over the dusty junk-filled barn, Louise, wearing her multi-coloured headscarf, arrived with Lian Meng and joined them. No one, including Wendy, was impressed.

Brian felt their disappointment hovering. "It's a bit messy," he said apologetically, "but it's yours if you can use it."

Wendy, forever determined her quest should come to fruition, took a deep breath. "Brian, it's going to be fine and we thank you."

There were nods of agreement all around. Also, some murmurs and mumbles that were not exactly intelligible.

Brian, pleased with what he gathered was a positive reaction, slipped his arm around Emily and smiled at her and nodded. "There are a few draughty cracks here and there; I'll fix those before you move in," he said cheerfully.

"Again, thanks, Brian," said Wendy, "that would be great."

"Right, I'll leave you ladies, to it." He gave Emily a peck on the cheek, which produced a giggle from her, and he left.

Wendy again took a deep breath and stood tall. After a moment's contemplation, she turned to the ladies. "Okay, first things first. You have all at some stage done some singing of sorts. Choir mainly. Right?"

Dot spoke up, "*No* . . . I don't sing, I sew, as discussed."

Louise raised her hand gingerly. "As discussed, I don't sing, but I will play the piano for rehearsal and help out in general."

Wendy nodded. "As discussed, right." She continued, "We still need one more."

"I have an idea," said Louise. "Alyson Cameron, she was with the Ampthill Players, did *Cabaret* two-three years back. She played Sally Bowles and was very good."

"I see," said Lian excitedly, "she Sally Bowles, she was old Sally Bowles, but she very good."

"She was good," agreed Wendy. "You're right and she's the only black Sally Bowles I have ever seen. God, I feel guilty . . . I haven't talked to or seen her in what must be three or four months! Have any of you seen her?"

There was a shaking of heads all around but for Kay. "I haven't seen her but Jan Clemens who directs the Players told me she dropped out of the Players a long time back."

"Really," said Wendy. "Well she's coming up to our age now," laughed Wendy. "And old enough to be thought of as a chocolate teapot. "I've known Alyson for years. We sang together at the Christmas Rotary Club dinner and dance, remember?"

"I do," said Arlene, "that was a fun night."

"It was that," recalled Wendy. "I also remember Alyson and I sang to Tim her husband on his birthday the year before last."

"I helped with the costumes for *Cabaret*," said Dot. "The director, Jan Clemens, didn't want her because of her age but she had the best voice by far. She has to be in her fifties."

"More like sixty," added Arlene.

"Ampthill Players sold record tickets with *Cabaret*," said Jan.

"Money, money, money," laughed Kay.

Then, in good voice, Lian Meng sang aloud the lyrics to 'Money Makes The World Go Around' from *Cabaret*.

Wendy joined Lian in the song.

The laughter was contagious. "Listen, listen," hollered Wendy. "I'll go see Alyson and get her on board, good thinking, Louise. Girls gather round." Wendy found an empty box, turned it upside down and, sat. The others secured similar seating. "If we can get Alyson we are set . . ."

" . . .To make fools of ourselves," remarked Kay. "You never said we were going to be doing public performances."

Wendy looked at her and shrugged. "Kay, what did you think we were going to do, sing to ourselves? The whole point in doing this is to let the world know we're not finished the day we become seniors." Wendy sighed and shook her head. "We all agreed did we not? That

most of the time we're treated as old age pensioners."
There were murmurs of agreement. "We've all tried to
pick up extra money to help out with the pension right?"
Again agreement. "We're treated as if we're suffering
from total infirmity. Others think we're hard of hearing
and shout platitudes. '*Are you alright, love, be careful
that's heavy, you better sit down and put your feet up,*'
the list goes on. I don't want to be on that list."

The ladies looked from one to another.

Jan came to the fore. "Agreed, but, Wendy, in
public?"

"Yes," yelled Wendy. "You sang in a choir, that's
public! Trust me, I will not let you embarrass yourselves,
any of you, I promise."

"Wendy," said Arlene. "It's alright for you. You've
sung with bands for years."

Emily joined the others. "It's a bit frightening,
Wendy."

Again there were mumblings of agreement all around
until Lian Meng said out loud, "I think we can do it."

Wendy raised an eyebrow and looked at each in turn.
"Well, a show of hands?"

After what seemed a lifetime the hands went up, not

all together but one at a time with some hesitation . . . but up they went making it unanimous.

Wendy smiled. "All in agreement."

"All for one and one for all," said Arlene. She smiled at Wendy. "You've done it again, Wen."

"Don't call me Wen, you know I hate it."

Arlene pulled her finger across the mouth as if to zip it. "Sorry," she said knowing full well she loathed being called Wen.

"Alright," shouted Wendy. "We need to work out a roster. One: for cleaning this place up. Two: rehearsal times."

Everyone pitched in with their ideas, all talked at once.

Chapter Seventeen

The barn project was a call for all hands on deck, except for Wendy's Ray, who was still in the dark about her new entrepreneurial venture. She had tried to convince herself *and* the others it was going to be a big surprise when Ray found out and she was fairly sure he would love it. Everyone had heard Arlene repeat over and over her thoughts on the outcome, '*tears at bedtime*', once again.

* * *

Over the next three days, husbands, Gary, Ken and Frank arrived and departed with cars carrying all types of cleaning paraphernalia. Brian repaired loose planking and broken windows. The ladies swept, dusted, vacuumed and moped. Emily handed out refreshments while Phil ran a water line to the only sink in the building. If the ladies needed to spend a penny they had to use the one outside at the back of the workshop. All in all, it had become a senior citizens' workforce, without complaint and still a work in progress.

Chapter Eighteen

Wendy's Smarty Pants pulled in behind the late model Ford compact parked in front of the Cameron home in Woburn Close. Wendy climbed out and headed down the gravel path with lawn and flower beds on either side. The red brick cottage was originally a farmhand cottage belonging to the Duke of Bedford's Woburn Estate. She rang the bell set in the middle of the green front door. A moment later Sue, an attractive African Caribbean woman in her thirties, opened the door.

Wendy smiled. "Hello, Sue . . ."

" . . . Mrs Knight?" Sue greeted with surprise.

"That's right, Wendy, please."

"God that's so weird," said Sue, "strange weird. I was *just* looking at your picture, you and Mum, it's on our dresser. Come in please."

Wendy stepped into the hall. Sue closed the door behind her and led the way through an open door. Wendy followed.

"Look who's here," called Sue as they entered the nicely furnished, neat, and spotless sitting room.

Alyson, an attractive black woman with a trim figure, not looking her sixty years stood next to her husband Tim, who was seated in a wheelchair. She smiled at Wendy.

Wendy's eyes went to Tim, she remembered him as a vibrant handsome black man, although in his sixties he had a head of tight curly grey hair – now, but for the hair, he was unrecognisable slumped in the wheelchair. He looked frail, his glossy black skin now ashen.

Before Wendy arrived, Alyson had been midway through changing Tim's Oxygen bottle. "*Wendy*, I don't believe it," she said as she carried on the necessary task of changing the oxygen. She snapped the hose into the neck of the bottle and the airflow was back and working. She moved to Wendy and hugged her.

"Alyson, you're a sight for sore eyes," exclaimed Wendy hugging her back.

Sue grabbed the photo frame from the dresser and handed it to Wendy. "This is the photograph with you and Mum at the Christmas show."

Alyson moved to look at the photograph in Wendy's hand. *She loved the photograph of herself and Wendy arm-in-arm, wearing radiant smiles*. "Wish we looked like that now."

Wendy jokingly jabbed Alyson with her elbow. "We do, we do. That's what I've come to talk to you about." Wendy turned her attention to Tim.

Alyson took the point. "Tim, I'm sorry, babe . . .. Look who's here." She moved to his side and adjusted the nasal airflow dispenser.

"Wendy, good memories," he said, his voice weak. "One of the happiest memories I have is of you two singing together on my birthday." Tim nodded repeatedly.

"I remember," said Wendy with purposeful excitement. "God that was a fun night, I think I wound up having too much to drink."

"So did we all," replied Alyson. "Sit yourself down. What brings you here, it's been so long?"

"I know," Wendy groaned as she sat on the sofa next to Tim's wheelchair. "I've been so busy . . . I know that's no excuse, but days just fly by and every time I turn around it's Friday."

Alyson sat on the footstool next to Tim. "I know what you mean," she agreed.

"Well," said Wendy as she looked from one to the

other. "The short and the tall of it is I want to know if you'd like to come and sing?"

For a moment Alyson's face lit up, and she looked at Tim, placing her hand on his. "I'm a bit past it now," she chuckled.

Wendy shook her. "Alyson, that's the point we are going to make, we're not past it."

"We?" Alyson questioned.

"Yes, we," Wendy said with enthusiasm, "all our old mates, you know everyone. Let me tell you what *we* put-out-to-grass seniors are up to. For a start, we are not going to be treated like chocolate teapots."

Tim laughed, which set off a coughing bout. Once under control, he laughed again.

Sue chuckled. "Chocolate teapot? I've never heard that before, why a chocolate teapot?"

"Because it's useless," answered Tim.

"Damned right," replied Wendy, "and we're not, and we are going to show them!"

Alyson eyed Wendy. "*We, them* . . . Wendy Knight, what are you up to?"

Wendy looked from one to the other. "I'll tell you what we have in mind."

Chapter Nineteen

As Ray and Rebecca pushed their cart with two bags of lawn fertiliser across the B&Q parking lot, something caught Ray's eye. Phil was strapping lengths of PVC pipe onto his roof rack. "There's Phil."

Rebecca followed his look and saw their next-door neighbour, Mr Roberts.

Ray changed direction with the cart and headed toward Phil's car. Once in range, he called out, "Hi, Phil."

Phil looked over the roof of his car. *He knew he was on the spot.* "Morning. Hi, Rebecca."

"Hello, Mr Roberts," she said, forgetting that the barn project, which she was privy to, was still a secret to be kept from her dad.

Ray brought the fertiliser cart to a stop behind Phil's car. "Where've you been hiding, Phil? Haven't seen you or Dot in days."

Phil continued strapping the pipe to the roof rack. "I'm doing a favour for a friend over in Flitwick . . . putting in a new heater."

"You should have called me, I'd have given you a hand."

"Bless you, Ray. No, it's okay he was wanting to do his bit, so he took a few days off to help me out."

"And Dot? I haven't seen her in ages," said Ray.

Phil knew he was getting in deep with Wendy's big surprise, as she was calling it! *Why were they all going along with it?* he asked himself. *Ray was his mate. Wendy had convinced herself and everyone else to keep him in the dark, and they were all going along with it, like a load of naughty children.*

"She's been at the centre," lied Phil, yet again.

Ray nodded. "Like Wendy. See you later, Phil." And he and Rebecca moved off toward their car.

"Yes . . . bye for now, bye, Rebecca," said Phil securing the last piece of piping on the roof rack and climbing into his car.

As Ray and Rebecca loaded the bags of fertiliser into the trunk of the car, Phil drove by tooting his horn. They both waved back as he drove by.

"On the way home from school, I saw Granny and Mr Roberts going into the old barn, down by Park," said Rebecca.

Ray closed the boot, thoughtfully looking at his granddaughter.

Chapter Twenty

Over the last fifteen minutes, as they drank coffee, Wendy had given Alyson and Sue an outline of her plan for the gang. The plan was not to be thought of as being ready for the scrap heap. But to show the world they were all still young enough to take on new projects.

Tim had listened intently, and at one juncture pointed out, "That's what happened to me at the brickyard."

Wendy took a breath. "And that's about it," she said looking at Tim. He smiled at her, and she noted it was the first time he had smiled since she arrived.

"It sounds great to me," said Tim.

Alyson put her empty coffee cup on the side table. "I'm your age, Wendy, and I'm not over the hill – I really would like to join you and the others, but I don't have the time, my days are full."

"She works two jobs, plus looking after me," Tim said looking up at Alyson.

"Talking of jobs, Mum." Sue looked at her watch.

Alyson also glanced at her watch. "I have to run Sue to work."

Wendy made to stand, but Tim reached over and rested his hand on Wendy's arm signalling her not to leave. "Finish your coffee," he said.

Wendy caught his drift. "I will, nice coffee."

"I have to go," said Alyson. "Good luck with the venture, Wendy. We really must get together soon." With that, she headed for the door concerned that she was going to make Sue late.

Sue followed. "Bye, Mrs Knight," she said backing out of the room, as she signalled Wendy to stay.

Confused, Wendy called, "Bye, Sue . . . and it's Wendy." The front door closed leaving Tim and Wendy alone.

Tim was fatigued and took two deep breaths. "Wendy, leave this to me. This is just what Alyson needs. She does two jobs, but not in the evenings. I can manage on my own up to a point. If I'm in need Sue can look out for me."

Wendy eyed him with suspicion. "Tim, I don't know . . . I don't want to make problems for you and the family."

"Wen," said Tim.

Wendy winced but broke her rule of a lifetime, by not snapping '*Don't call me Wen.*'

Tim gave her a big smile. "I was a great fan of the movies. I mean going to the movies. Not like now, putting in a disc or streaming and flopping back on the sofa and falling to sleep halfway through the film."

Wendy laughed. "I know what you mean."

"I had heroes but didn't heed their warnings. Do you remember in America, John Wayne in the 1970s said, '*Stop smoking it's killing me*.' Then in the 80s, Yul Brynner told us the same, '*Smoking is a killer, it's killing me*.' Now it's killing me, Wendy. With Alyson working two jobs to whittle down the medical bills I've piled up. She takes me to private doctors for treatments etc. We're in debt £7,300."

Wendy grimaced. "God, Tim, I'm sorry to hear that."

"The brickyard laid eighty of us off three years ago. Since then it's been odd employment here and there, but as you see I can't do it any longer." Tim coughed and flopped back in the chair his eyes closed.

"Are you alright?" Wendy asked, concerned, his eyes were still closed she had no idea what to do if he was having an attack.

Tim opened his eyes much to Wendy's relief. "Yes . . . yes, it comes and goes, don't worry I'm not going to conk out on you," he chuckled. "I don't want this messing the rest of Alyson's life up. She's *going* to be at your barn for your singing group; she was born to sing. This is just the thing she needs."

Wendy thought about what Tim was saying. "Tim . . . it would be great if she joined us. But I don't want her feeling . . ."

Tim smiled. "Guilty. Wen, Alyson, and I have faced it, *along with* Sue. I don't have much time left, but I would like to see my darling enjoy what time we have left. And God willing, to see her up on the stage singing with you girls would be wonderful for us all."

Wendy nodded her head. "You had better not be lying to me, Tim Cameron, I'll come find you and haunt you no matter where you've gone."

Tim cackled. "I've already told her she has to sing at my funeral, so you better get her in practice."

Wendy laughed. "I will, God willing, and I'll sing along with her . . . I'm sorry I didn't mean . . ."

" . . . Hush," replied Tim.

"'Over The Rainbow'? Alyson told me that's your favourite, it's mine too."

Tim straightened himself in the chair. "That's it. We

have a date. At my funeral, you two singing 'Over The Rainbow'." Then out of the blue, he asked, "How's Ray doing?"

Relieved to change the subject Wendy answered, "He's fine. Bored with retirement, but fine."

Tim smiled. "I bet he's still talking about your legs."

Wendy was surprised. "What about my legs?"

Tim laughed. "He always said you had great legs."

"I'll give him great legs," she said not able to hide the smile." Wendy stood. "I'd better get going. You look after yourself, Tim." She moved toward the door. At the door she turned back; he was already asleep with a smile on his face. She moved back to him and kissed him on the forehead, saying quietly, "See you on opening night." She left closing the front door quietly.

Chapter Twenty-One

The interior of the barn was now in much better shape, which excited Wendy. She was dying to start rehearsing the girls. Brian's assortment of wood of all shapes and sizes, plus his broken oddments of discarded furniture, had been moved to the far end of the barn and covered with a tarpaulin. This left them 30 X 40 feet where they could rehearse and set up whatever they needed. Plus they had a sink with running water, to which Phil was now making the final adjustments underneath. Next to the sink, they had set up a table with an assortment of mugs and the makings for coffee or tea and, of course, a tea kettle. Dot had arranged a curtain around the refreshment area hiding it from the rehearsal area of the barn.

Brian, with the help of Louise, Kay and Lian, was setting up Louise's keyboard in the front corner of their working space. Wendy watched them manoeuvre the keyboard to Louise's liking lost in thought. *Wendy knew from her experience, her acapella ensemble had to start with an accompaniment, singing along with the music would get the timing and the sound they were wanting into their heads. They would hear the melody and the timing. Louise's offering to play for them was going to be a lifesaver. In the beginning, they could be guided by Louise at the keyboard, then when she was sure it was embedded in everyone's head and they knew the programme of songs to be sung . . . Then work would start, without Louise and her keyboard.*

* * *

Wendy snapped out of her daydream and went to work cleaning the dust and grit from the ten folding chairs she had borrowed from the senior centre.

Emily readied coffee and biscuits for the workers alongside Phil still with his head under the sink. Suddenly, the water pipe Phil was installing separated from the adjoining collar and water sprayed up and over the curtain.

Louise and Kay used their bodies to protect and shield the keyboard, while Phil ran to turn off the water.

Lian grabbed some rags off of the chair by the door and, although getting soaked, she fought her way behind the curtain and under the sink and tried to block the gap in the pipe with the rags. *Try being the operative word.*

Jan tried to help and went to the rescue of Lian but

was beaten back by a jet of very cold water in her face.

Arlene retreated toward the back of the barn next to the tarpaulin.

Wendy ran toward the fountain of water coming from behind the curtain when suddenly it stopped. Phil had turned off the water at the main.

Emily, Lian and Jan were drenched, and not very happy ladies. Wendy turned her back on them to hide the smile that was about to change to laughter.

Chapter Twenty-Two

That evening at home Wendy felt especially guilty about not sharing the day's adventures with Ray. He and Wendy relaxed in the sitting room, Ray at one end of the sofa watching *Coronation Street* volume down low. Wendy sat on the other end – feet up on his lap – and flipped through the pages of a magazine. She paused scanning the pages and looked at the TV . . . She looked at Ray.

"You can't hear what they're saying, it's too low," she said and motioned toward the television.

"It's okay, not watching really," he said, eyes still on the TV.

Wendy lowered the magazine. "Then turn it off, love, or find something else to watch."

Ray fished between the cushions and found the remote and turned off the television. Ray turned to face her. "How was the centre today?"

Wendy faked focus back on the magazine and mumbled, "Fine."

Ray lifted her feet from his lap, stood and moved across the room, leaned on the piano, and looked out through the window into the night.

"Rebecca and I saw Phil at B&Q today," he said.

"Yeah – Did Rebecca have a good day helping out?"

"Yes . . . Phil says he's doing a private job."

Wendy didn't like the feel of where this conversation was going" . . . Keeping himself busy I guess."

Ray turned from the window and looked at her. "He said Dot was at the centre."

Wendy now really felt uncomfortable. "Dot's here there and everywhere."

Ray moved back to the sofa and stood facing Wendy. "As far as I know, we've never had secrets, right?"

Wendy needed a way out. She laughed. "*Ha-ha*, as far as you know."

"Cut the comedy, Wendy . . . You've been lying to me."

Wendy looked at him. "No, not lying," she managed to say.

Ray without taking his eyes off her sat back down on the sofa. "I asked how was the centre today – you haven't been there, I called."

"I didn't say I'd been there. I said it was fine."

"And Dot! What about Dot?"

"What about her? I never said I saw her, I never lied."

"Then what are you up to?" asked Ray, now angry.

Wendy let out a sigh. "Oh, Ray! I've not told you a lie. I've just not told you everything I'm up to."

Ray shook his head in frustration. "That's as good as a lie, not telling me whatever it is you're concocting yet again."

"Not," said Wendy.

"Is," said Ray.

"Not," she repeated.

"Is," snapped back Ray.

They, as always, had reached a stalemate and the silence hung heavy. After a moment that seemed a lifetime, Ray folded his arms and stared at the blank television screen. More silent moments passed. Wendy moved a little closer to him. Still, silence prevailed – She now sidled up closer. "I'm guilty," she said, now ready to admit everything.

Ray looked at her. "It's Phil, isn't it?"

Wendy wrinkled her nose. "It's Phil what?"

"Rebecca saw you and him going into Brian's barn."

Wendy turned to him almost nose to nose. "*What . . . Do you think Phil Roberts and I are at it?*"

"Well?"

Wendy took his hands in hers. "My darling man. Starting a new singing class and not telling you about it . . . Yes guilty. But having an affair I am not."

She leaned forward, kissing him on the cheek, nose and lips. "The only affair I want is with you." She now kissed him fully on the lips.

Ray started to return the kiss – then suddenly shrank back.

"Singing class!" he yelled.

Wendy tried to reignite the kiss saying softly, "It was going to be a surprise."

Ray got to his feet and marched into the kitchen, and then came the sound of a drawer opening. He marched back into the room and dumped the pile of holiday magazines on her lap. "That's the surprise I want. Us going on holiday, our road trips, all the things we talked about. I'm going to bed."

Ray headed for the hall and up the stairs.

Wendy called, "A kiss good night is out of the question then?"

Ray's voice came back at her, "Yes."

Wendy called back, "I heard that."

Now she felt guilty, she slumped back on the sofa and thumbed through Ray's travel magazines that he had dumped on her lap.

Chapter Twenty-Three

Johanna pulled into the drive of number 2 Millbrook Lane. As she climbed out of the car Wendy came out of the house, clearly not in a good frame of mind. "Let's walk," she said and slipped her arm through Johanna's and led her out of the drive of Millbrook Lane.

"Mum?"

"Thanks for coming over," said Wendy, not hiding the fact that she was not a happy camper this morning.

Johanna looked at her. "Your text sounded as if you were in trouble."

"I need a good kick in the pants. I'm a dummy . . . Your mother's as thick as two short planks," said Wendy, now almost in tears.

Johanna tried to lighten the moment by saying, "True, and that's on a good day. What have you done this time? And why didn't you tell me?"

"Ha," said Wendy with an attempt to laugh. "You're joking. You couldn't keep a secret from the day you were born."

"That's not true!"

"Yes it is, you'll always blab to someone."

"You haven't done much better by the sound of it," said Johanna.

Wendy sighed, shaking her head. "You're right there. What a mess I've made of everything."

"Okay so tell me what you have done."

"I've never lied to your father or any of you," snapped back Wendy. "I may have danced around the truth, a little."

"I still don't know what truth you danced around, or what you never told me," said Johanna getting annoyed with her mother. Then the penny dropped, and she came to a halt and turned to face her. "You never told Dad about the Palladium or getting up on the stage and singing."

Wendy let out a sigh. "It's *worse* . . . I've formed a senior citizen singing group, without mentioning a word to your father."

"Mum, you're supposed to be retired and going to travel, big plans, vacations driving around the country, etc . . ."

" . . .. *I know* . . . I know – I got this bee in my bonnet about being sixty-plus and finished, sort of left behind."

Johanna started them walking again. "Mum, you are *not* left behind."

Wendy glanced across at her. "I'm getting older . . . How long do I have left? The clock keeps ticking, my darling. I've told you before, every time I turn around it's Friday."

Johanna squeezed Wendy's arm. "Mum, you'll go on forever."

Wendy again shook her head. "No my darling, I won't. None of us will. I look in the mirror and see the changes day by day. It frightens me. Remember Alyson and Tim Cameron?"

"Yes," said Johanna.

"I went to visit them yesterday. Tim hasn't long to live: emphysema, smoking."

Johanna shuddered. "Sorry to hear that. But, Mum, you don't smoke, you never have and you're as fit as a flea."

Wendy turned them around and headed back toward the house. "Who the hell told you fleas are fit, how do you know?" Wendy said somewhat brighter. "Come on I'll make us breakfast."

"And Dad?" asked Johanna.

"He's gone out."

"He'll be back," said Johanna.

"He better, or I'll never talk to him again," added Wendy.

"You won't be able to if he never comes back!"

Wendy nodded. "Purely a technicality."

Johanna gave her mum a dig in the ribs with her elbow as they turned into the drive.

Chapter Twenty-Four

Arlene had volunteered to get breakfast for the barn clean-up gang: Bacon and Egg McMuffins. Two youngsters held the door of McDonald's open for Arlene as she manoeuvred her way out carrying three boxes holding the seven Bacon and Egg McMuffins. Seven medium cups of coffee were dangerously balanced on top of the boxes. The need for coffee was because the coffee percolator loaned by Kay was not working as of yesterday afternoon. Head down concentrating on the balancing act, Arlene made her way carefully toward her car, two of the cups teetered, edging toward disaster.

"Let me help," a voice called to her from between two parked cars.

Arlene looked up. "O*h my God it's Ray*," she heard herself saying under her breath.

Ray relieved her of the two teetering cups and managed to save a third from falling to the ground.

"Oh, hello, Ray, fancy seeing you here," was the first thing that came into her head, *and it sounded pretty dumb,* she realised as soon as the words were out of her mouth.

"Good job I came when I did, you were about to lose your coffee."

"I was that, bless you," said Arlene. "Where you off to, Ray?"

"I came out for breakfast for a change. Where's your car?" he asked.

Arlene knew she had guilt written across her face and it was Wendy's fault. She swallowed, which she was sure Ray must have heard, she'd heard it! "At the end of the row, I couldn't park any nearer," she managed to blurt out. "Thanks, Ray."

"You're welcome," he said. "They burgers?"

"No, Bacon and Egg McMuffins."

"Two boxes!" Ray smiled, he was enjoying his moment. But not for one minute did he think that Arlene would give up Wendy and her secret.

Arlene's mind was racing for an explanation! What was coming next? *Where the hell was she supposed to be going this time in the morning with two boxes of Bacon and Egg McMuffins and seven cups of coffee?*

"I hear Bacon and Egg McMuffins are good for the vocal cords," said Ray.

"No. I . . ." She stopped in her tracks and looked him in the eye . . .. "You *know*, Wendy told you?"

"No. I water-boarded her until she talked."

Arlene could now breathe freely, she exhaled to prove it to herself.

"I'm . . . we're all going to be relieved you know," she said.

They made their way toward the end of the row and her car. "So you had to torture her?"

"Only a little," answered Ray.

Chapter Twenty-Five

Johanna looked at her mother across the kitchen table as they sipped their coffee. "So you've taken on the coaching of five old biddies to become entertainers."

"*See*, there you go with the *old* again!" snapped Wendy.

"Just a figure of speech, Mum."

"To you yes, to me it hurts, and the other old biddies."

"*Mum*. they didn't *know* they were old until you told them *and* talked them into this troupe of singing vagabonds."

Wendy grimaced. "Stop it, you know it's a good idea."

They fell silent. Wendy stared out of the kitchen window, and Johanna drank coffee and thumbed through the holiday magazines on the table where Wendy had left them last night.

"What time did Dad go out?"

Wendy drank coffee. "Early," she said.

Johanna looked at her. "So you've commandeered Brian's barn, you've left your troupe of girls down there cleaning the place up and you've decided to take the day off."

"No," said Wendy. "I called Arlene and told her I had some loose ends to tie up. Besides most of the clean-up has been done; it's only the final touches they're doing today."

"The loose ends being that Dad has found you out, right?" said Johanna at the same time she noticed something on the dresser. She stood and moved to the dresser. It was a music box, she picked it up. "I haven't seen this for years."

Wendy turned to look. "For the past thirty-odd years that's lived on my dressing table," she said heavyhearted.

Johanna set it down on the table.

"Your father must have brought it down."

Johanna looked at the music box, and then at her mother. "He's been remembering."

Wendy picked up the music box. "The last song I performed with the band that night was at the Savoy Grill . . . your father was there. I sang 'My Foolish Heart'. My retiring song after a twelve-year run of band work." Tears formed in her eyes. "After the show, he took me to the Ivy restaurant in Covent Garden for supper – he gave me this." She held the little music box in both hands. Tears filled her eyes as she stood and moved through into the sitting room with the music box.

* * *

In the sitting room, Wendy moved to the piano and sat at the keyboard. She placed the music box on the piano in front of her.

Johanna stood at the doorway and leaned back against the door frame. Moments passed and Wendy lifted the lid of the music box . . . the little box started to play 'My Foolish Heart'.

Wendy listened to the first few bars, then accompanied it note for note on the piano, and she sang softly.

Johanna watched and listened from the doorway, she now had the start of tears in her eyes.

Sensing movement behind her, she turned her head to see her dad holding a box of doughnuts. His finger went to his lips. Shush, he signalled and sidled up to his daughter and listened to Wendy's dulcet tones; they brought back wonderful memories that were close to his heart. The accompaniment of the soft gentle music box and the piano made time stand still.

Ray and his daughter leaned against each other in the doorway, the box of doughnuts between . . . and enjoyed the moment.

"Oh yeah," Ray heard himself say involuntarily. He moved to Wendy with doughnuts in hand. She stopped playing.

Ray shook his head. "No, don't stop." He placed the doughnuts on the piano next to the music box. Wendy smiled and continued as Johanna walked over to the sofa.

Wendy continued singing.

Ray sat on the piano stool next to her.

The music box was long silent and the last note from the piano faded as Ray kissed Wendy on the cheek.

"Doughnuts?" asked Ray.

Teary-eyed, Wendy looked at him.

"How long have you been there?"

She looked at Johanna on the sofa. "Did you know he was there?"

Johanna shrugged. "No," she lied.

Ray raised an eyebrow. "Good voice for a forty-year-old."

Wendy gave him a peck on the cheek. "You wish – I'm sorry about everything, love."

Ray kissed her gently, this time on the lips. "Doughnuts?" He looked at Johanna. "Johanna?"

Johanna shook her head, "I don't think I should be here, au revoir." She blushed as she headed for the door and home.

Ray slipped his arm around Wendy's shoulder and hugged her close. "I can't win can I? You're never going to put your feet up."

Wendy took a doughnut from the box on the piano and took a large bite, filling her mouth. She then said, unintelligibly, "Humm, hum..ha humm ha humm."

Ray shook his head. He closed and opened the music box, and 'My Foolish Heart' started to play again. He stood and held out his hand, Wendy took his hand in hers and stood, the remains of the doughnut still in her other hand. Ray took her in his arms and they danced. After a moment Wendy, mouth still full of doughnut, again said something unintelligible.

Ray smiled. "I don't think much of your singing."

She punched him on the arm, then demolished the remains of the doughnut. Still incoherent she muttered, "Humm, humm ha hmm."

"What's that? You want to take me to bed this time of day!"

Again she thumped him . . . but let him lead her

toward the stairs, remains of doughnut still between her fingers.

Chapter Twenty-Six

Jan stepped into the barn followed by Kay and Dot arm-in-arm. Behind them, Lian entered smiling from ear to ear. Louise, Arlene, and Emily brought up the rear. In turn, they slipped off their coats and hung them on Phil's makeshift cloak rack to the right of the door. One by one they turned and looked at the results of the three days of hard work they had put in. Their now-to-be workspace, from the door to the tarpaulin that covered all of Phil's odds and ends and bits and pieces, had been cleaned, scrubbed and dusted, and was now finished and ready for whatever.

"You wouldn't know it was the same place," mused Arlene.

Jan walked to the chair next to Louise's keyboard and sat. "It looks so good I may move in."

All agreed and the chatter started up but was short-lived. "Morning all," Wendy yelled as she emerged from the walkway between the wall and the tarpaulin at the back of the barn. She wore black slacks and a red shirt. They all watched as she moved along the wall of the barn and fed out an electric cable, tucking it in against the wall. Finally, she connected it to a six-outlet electrical surge box on the floor underneath Louise's keyboard already plugged in. Next, she plugged in two of the three microphones on their stands, the third one was a hand microphone, she plugged that into the box. The ladies exchanged looks, and Emily giggled. Connecting up, Wendy turned and faced them, all staring at her in silence, Emily stopped her giggle.

"What?" said Wendy.

"What?" echoed Jan.

"*So*?" asked Kay.

Wendy repeated herself, "What?"

"You know what," said Dot. "Ray knows . . . Right?"

Wendy made as if she was checking the microphone connections, and fiddled with the cables. "Certainly, he knows. I told you I'd tell him when the time was right."

Kay mimicked Wendy, "*This is a secret, Ray mustn't know.*"

"Very funny." Wendy planted her hands on her hips. "How did you know he knew?"

Arlene stepped up. "I bumped into him as I was coming out of McDonald's carrying six Bacon and Egg

McMuffins and six coffees, he held the door open for me. On seeing him my heart missed a beat; I almost dropped the lot. He saved the coffees going to the ground, and then he walked me to the car. En route, he asked me what was in the box, and I told him." Arlene gave Wendy her puppy-dog look. "He said he'd heard Bacon and Egg McMuffins were good for the vocal cords. With that I knew the cat was out of the bag . . . either you'd told him or he'd guessed something was going on."

"Well we're all happier he knows," said Jan.

"Ditto," agreed Arlene, "you put us all on the spot."

Wendy gave a nod. "You're right and I'm sorry . . . But he's okay with it . . . at the moment!"

"What does that mean?" asked Emily.

Wendy bent down and inspected the plug going into the keyboard to avoid eye contact with Emily. "He's okay with it at the moment. Right, no more chit-chat." She stood and faced them. "Wipe the smile off of your faces, let's get to work."

Dot announced she was going to get coffee and headed for the alcove.

Wendy turned on the microphones giving them a tap check, all were working.

Louise adjusted her keyboard stool and sat. At the same moment, the door opened and Alyson stepped in. Wendy's face lit up. She rushed over to Alyson and hugged her, then turned back to the group. "For those of you that don't know her already, welcome Alyson Cameron."

Lian seemed to be the only one who didn't know Alyson but quickly introduced herself, whilst there were hellos and hugs from the others. Even Dot made it back from the alcove for a quick hug.

Alyson took Wendy aside. "When I got home Tim got onto me. He wanted me to join in."

"That's great," said Wendy, already knowing Tim's feelings on the subject.

"He was truly adamant about me being part of the group," said Alyson seeming to want to assure Wendy it was alright for her to be there.

"Good, the important thing is you are here," said Wendy.

"Wendy, I have to leave at two. I start my shift at 2:30." Alyson smiled and gave Wendy another hug.

Wendy laughed. "Alyson, it's alright, whatever time you have is fine; you're going to be the most experienced anyway. Besides, we'll all have had enough by 2:30 I'm sure. Now relax and enjoy." Wendy went to her bag hanging on the wall peg and took out photocopied pages of 'Do-Re-Mi', sheet music from *The Sound of Music*. She handed them out and moved and stood between the two microphones. The ladies looked at the sheet music, and then at each other.

Arlene smiled. "Oh my . . . 'Do-Re-Mi'!"

Wendy nodded. "We have to start somewhere. I'm sure you all know it but you have the song sheet just in case. This will give us an idea of our range."

"Wendy, why do we have to be acapella?" asked Emily. "We have Louise with her piano."

Wendy bit her bottom lip while she thought about the question. "Sit yourselves down, I'll share my thoughts with you."

The ladies found themselves a seat and turned them to face Wendy as Dot arrived with mugs of coffee and handed them around, then took a seat next to Kay.

"We are going to be seven voices . . . *Yes*, one instrument could accompany us but we'd swamp it," she explained. "We would need three or four . . . keyboard, guitar, bass, brass and maybe string."

"That's five," said Emily.

"*Shut up,* Emily," snapped Wendy.

Emily shrugged and muffled her near giggle with a closed fist against her mouth.

Wendy continued. "We are going to show ourselves and others we are *not* past it. We are going to give enjoyment to the ones that need it – We're going to bring entertainment to their lives, *right*?"

There was agreement all around.

"*Emily*, to answer your question," said Wendy, "if we are going to entertain hospitals, senior citizens' centres and other groups that can't afford entertainment . . . We have to afford to be able to do it. And we can't do that carrying around four" – she looked to Emily – "*or* five musicians, they are not going to work for free. Hence acapella. We need Louise to keep us in the right key and get us all used to our music. When we are ready, she will drop out and we will be on our own." She held her hand out toward Louise in appreciation.

Louise nodded her thanks, as did Alyson with a hand clap which was taken up by the others. Wendy joined in.

Once everyone had quietened, Wendy once again took the floor. "Singing acapella can be a daunting task as a beginner to singing. That's why we need to make sure our voices can sing properly, again over to Louise who will give us our keys and range. Most times the best way to do this is through a professional vocal coach – but they're super expensive, fifty to a hundred pounds per session, but you have one free: *me, that's what I do*. I'm going to be your ticket to vocal control, a smooth tone and pitch, also the ability to hit both high and low notes effectively. Some of you are more than halfway there, you've been to my classes many times, and the others have sung in the choir so you all have a good start. Once I put the polishing touch to the control of your voice we will be singing acapella to perfection."

"We hope," said Kay doubtfully.

"Oh yee of little faith," laughed Wendy.

"Did you know that the closest anyone ever comes to perfection is on a job application?" said Kay.

"Haha," answered Wendy. "Trust me, we are going to be perfect."

Jan looked at the song sheet in her hand, her face lit up. "'Do-Re-Mi', I used to sing along with Julie Andrews whenever I heard her sing this."

"Good," Wendy hollered, "you can sing along with us

now."

"I know 'Do-Re-Mi'," Lian called out.

"You would, clever clogs," said Arlene with a smile.

"Ladies we have to start someplace. Louise . . ." said Wendy.

"Right," Louise answered and readied herself.

Arlene waved her song sheet. "If Julie Andrews and the children can do it so can we!"

Wendy got to her feet. "Right, that's the spirit, three at each microphone."

The ladies teamed up from left to right. Arlene, Jan, Kay, then Lian, Alyson and Emily.

"I'm going to mess it up. I will lose the tempo . . . I always do," Arlene whinged.

Wendy came to the rescue. "No, you won't. Listen to Louise, she will keep us on track, and all of *you*, keep your eyes on me." She stepped back into a conducting position in front of the ladies, microphone in her hand. "Arlene will start us off and we'll go through once to blow the cobwebs off. Then we'll take a second run. Then togetherness, right . . ."

No response from the ladies!

"Ladies, right?" Wendy shouted. She knew she was

going to have to do a lot of coaxing to build their confidence – *change of tactic.*' "Right, ladies?" she repeated softly, rather than her gung-ho approach. It worked.

"Right," was the loud response all around.

"Great." Wendy smiled, "any stumbles or mishaps, don't worry." Wendy nodded to Louise at the keyboard. "Starting with a C for Arlene if you please." Louise went into a brief intro. Wendy with her free hand led the tempo. On the eighth note of Louise's introduction, she hit a C and Wendy pointed to Arlene. She took her cue and launched into 'Do-Re-Mi', a touch shaky on the first three lyrics.

Wendy cued Jan, who sang loud, but she was okay.

She then cued Kay, who was on the money.

Lian took her cue, Also in good voice.

Alyson was on cue and good. Wendy beamed.

Emily jumped on her cue slightly ahead of Louise.

Wendy cued Arlene again. Arlene had now found her voice and confidence.

Wendy cued Jan again, concluding their first run through.

Wendy spun around and threw her hand in the air.

"You're all doing fine. Kay, away you go." There were big smiles all around, they had surprised themselves. Now, with a second wind, they were off and this time much more confident.

Wendy was over the moon. "Much better . . . One more time." And they did, with zest.

* * *

Over the coming months, Wendy kept a tight rein on everyone and everything, and it was not an easy task. She taught them voice control, pitch, and harmony, she rode them hard, they complained, called her a heartless bully, and worse. But then there was a lot of laughter and merriment, more than despair. On top of all this, everyone had their agendas. All had families that had to be taken into consideration, and even though they had all signed off on the fact the group was going to happen, it *still* had to happen and Wendy was at the helm.

The one with the biggest problem was Lian Meng. She ran her Chinese Takeaway six days a week, Tuesday through Sunday, with the occasional help of a son and two daughters. Lian's husband had left her two years ago for a woman bus driver from Bedford who was a bingo caller in her spare time! Her children decided it was important for their mum to join the group as she loved to sing. So, they worked it out. Lian did the morning pre-cook on rehearsal days and the children took over the running on those days *and* the one evening at the weekend.

Emily had always done charity work and volunteered much of her time at the senior centre, so she had to juggle to make her time fit, *and* she did.

Alyson was holding down two jobs and looking after Tim. Between him and their daughter, Sue, they made sure she was there for ninety-five per cent of the rehearsals.

Everyone else seemed to make it work week-in-week-out.

Dot beavered away at home with costumes and was very seldom seen at a rehearsal.

Wendy, after listening to everybody's whys and wherefores, had set the rehearsal times. Two afternoons a week and an evening over the weekend and everything fell into place and ticked over nicely. Over the weeks of rehearsals, the support that came from the husbands and children was outstanding, through summer and into the autumn. Not one of the group could be called a

'*Chocolate Teapot*' and not one wore the label '*Out to Pasture*' . . . All had lots of life left in them yet and they had come through for her, Wendy had her acapella group and they were good.

* * *

Now Wendy thought back with hindsight – *It was she who got the bee in her bonnet about old age and being put out to pasture. What was it that Henry had said? 'No, out to pasture for me, that would be the end. No way back from that, retirement, to the grave.' Henry was right and after being back on that stage for 'Over The Rainbow', she knew sitting at home . . . she wasn't ready for it yet, if ever. She was not quite ready to join the other tourists on cruises and road trips as much as her darling Ray wanted. But they had been* her *thoughts, she had talked everybody else into it . . . they were quite happy going along as they were, but now because they were thinking chocolate teapots, not for them. Now because of her hang-up about old age, she had more or less forced them all into her mindset . . . she now had a singing group and it had to work and be good. 'Oh, Wendy', she said to herself what have you done!*

Chapter Twenty-Seven

It was Wendy's choice of restaurant for the family's regular monthly night out to dinner, they took turns choosing. Wendy, Ray, Johanna and Kevan sat at a window table in the Flitwick Manor's hotel dining room. Rebecca had elected to go to a movie in Bedford with her friend Patsy. Most times when it was Wendy's turn to choose, she chose the Manor, but that was never a problem as they all liked the country house hotel and its lovely dining room, with its wood panelling, candlelight, and views across the terrace to the floodlit gardens surrounding the lake, pricey, but good. Tonight there were twenty or so diners of varying ages, all happily enjoying their evening.

Wendy and the family had finished their meal and paused their discussion while coffee was served to them. Coffees all around, the waiter moved away.

"Mum," continued Johanna a touch upset, "you know you could have had time at the studio from the beginning of your rehearsals."

"Johanna, I turned the studio over to you and you use

it well," answered Wendy. "You're sweet, but Brian gave us the use of the barn and it's worked out well. As senior citizens, we are doing fine."

"Johanna . . . Don't let her pull you into the senior citizen's bit again," said Ray jokingly.

Wendy shook her head. "Ganging up on me."

Their waiter returned and presented the cheque. Kevan picked it up.

"Let's split it," offered Ray.

"No, it's our treat," said Johanna.

Kevan placed his credit card on the cheque, and the waiter took it and disappeared. Kevan looked at his watch. "We have to make a move. I'm stock-taking tomorrow; it's an early start for me." As they prepared to leave the waiter brought the cheque back and Kevan signed the credit slip.

Johanna kissed Wendy on the cheek. "Super dinner, Mum."

"Thanks to you two." Wendy smiled, standing. The others followed suit.

"Hey," said Johanna, "I forgot to say I'm sorry to hear about Alyson and Tim. I only just found out."

Wendy raised an eyebrow. "How did you know?

Alyson didn't want anyone to know!"

"Her daughter, Sue, we hadn't seen each other for a bit and yesterday we did a catch-up."

Wendy nodded. "I think Alyson would thank you if you kept it to yourself."

"I will, we'll talk to you tomorrow. Night, Dad." She gave him a peck on the cheek.

Wendy and Ray watched them leave the restaurant ahead of them. Ray looked at Wendy. "Alyson! What about her and Tim?"

Wendy exhaled. "Let's go to the music room and have a nightcap," she suggested. "I'll fill you in."

* * *

They were the only ones in the music room. Wendy had often wondered why it was so called, there was no piano or music of any kind in the spacious room. It was used mostly for pre-dinner drinks or nightcaps. They both ordered Drambuie on the rocks and sank into the sofa in front of the fireplace with its last remains of burning embers. Wendy moved closer to Ray and sidled into his shoulder. "Remember I told you Tim is very ill?" she reminded him. Ray nodded.

"Alyson paid for him to go private as she knew time

was important . . . they've piled up some big medical bills."

The waiter arrived with their Drambuies, and they sat in silence and sipped their drinks. Ray thought about what she had told him – "Don't they have private insurance from his work, he'd been there a long time?"

"It's unfair," said Wendy, "his insurance would only cover NHS. Alyson moved him over to a private consultant and treatment. I can understand that. I think she knows shc's grasping at straws . . . It's a matter of time. The trouble is because he was laid off from the brickyard two years back whatever insurance he had has run out. They're only just keeping their heads above water," she explained.

"Tell me about it," said Ray. "I dread to think about what's going to happen to our kids. They are saying the NHS could be exhausted and broke by 2040."

"That's a long time off, and things can change," Wendy muttered taking a sip of her drink.

"Time shoots by, my love," groaned Ray.

Wendy nodded. "Alyson's working two jobs, but I think it's getting too much for her." She smiled. "Last week she told Tim she was going to quit the group . . .

She was worried she was neglecting him, *he* wouldn't hear of her quitting."

Ray smiled and gave a nod. "That's the Tim I know."

They both sat silent, staring into the few glowing embers. Wendy turned and looked at him thoughtfully – "Ray, could we afford to help some?"

Ray turned to her, and after a moment he bit on his bottom lip as he turned her question over in his mind. "We can try. How much are they in the red?" he asked.

"£7,300 she said," Wendy replied, with hesitation.

Ray virtually did a double-take. "God almighty, Wendy! We can't find that sort of money. We just don't have it, you know that. This time next year could be a little different, our mortgage comes to an end, then we'll be debt-free."

Wendy knew he was right. "Do you think we could afford £200 or £300?"

Ray thought on it . . . "I wish I was a Richard Branson, I'd clean the slate for them. If we don't change your carpet in the hall until the end of the year, we could maybe make it five hundred."

She leaned across and kissed him on the cheek.

Ray sat back on the sofa and looked at her. "Darling,

you know Alyson, and I know Tim, they may not take to charity."

Wendy touched the tip of her forefinger to the side of her nose. "I'm not giving her a choice."

Ray raised an eyebrow and looked at her, he knew his wife, she had something up her sleeve as usual. "Okay, you do what you have to. I should go visit Tim . . . It's been a long time."

Wendy smiled. "He'd like that. And you two can talk about my legs."

Ray furrowed his brow. "What legs!"

"You know what legs." She finished her Drambuie, not bothering to hide her grin.

Chapter Twenty-Eight

Ray sat across from Tim, who was in his wheelchair, his oxygen nasal dispenser in place. He looked at Tim. "What legs? 'You know what legs,' he said."

Tim laughed and shook his head.

Ray managed to laugh but was finding it difficult, seeing his old friend in such poor health. He had not seen Tim in close to a year and he got a hell of a shock when Tim opened the door from his wheelchair; he hardly recognised him. Ray took a breath and embellished the tale. "'Her legs. The ones you talk to your buddies about.' I tell you, Tim, she gave me what for."

"Ray, believe me, I didn't say anything offensive about Wendy," answered Tim, concerned.

Ray smiled. "I know that. No, she was winding me up . . . she was joking, enjoying the moment if truth be told."

"I hope so," said Tim. "I'd hate to upset her."

Ray held up his hand in protest. "Tim, I promise you, far from it, she was enjoying it, I know my Wendy."

Tim nodded in relief.

"Tim, she thinks she may have put you on the spot

about this singing bee she has in her bonnet."

Tim shook his head. "No, the opposite, she nailed it. I meant what I said. It's great for me to see Alyson do something other than being at my beck and call day and night."

Ray settled back into his chair, more comfortable knowing Tim was not suffering because of Wendy. "From what I've heard she wouldn't have it any other way, Alyson's a good one."

"Ray, my friend, I've been sick for coming up to three years, she and our daughter Sue are at my side day and night." He was now having to take a breath between words. "Never . . . a . . . complaint . . . never . . . a cross word." He closed his mouth and took a few deep breaths through the nasal oxygen feed and continued talking. "Until Wendy got her involved with the singing, she'd never had a moment to herself – I always come first!"

"God, Tim, I know it's been a while, but the last time we were together you weren't in a wheelchair and gasping for breath."

"No, it's the last year that it's got this bad. I'll be lucky if I see Christmas."

The old friends sat in awkward silence until Tim

asked, "Ray, pour me some coffee."

He handed Ray his empty coffee mug and nodded toward the open kitchen where the coffee percolator sat on the unit.

Ray took the mug and went to the coffeemaker. "Doctors have been wrong before," said Ray as he poured coffee into Tim's mug. Mug filled, Ray moved back to Tim and handed him his coffee.

Tim took a sip. "Not this time. I know how I feel and it can only get worse. Hey, we *all* have to die sometime!"

Ray sat back in his chair facing his dying friend. Tim smiled. "It's inevitable, Ray. I'm not afraid. Alyson and Sue know that."

Ray nodded, thinking about what Tim had said. "I hear you . . . I don't think I'll be afraid when my time comes, but then I intend to stay around a long time if I can." Immediately he regretted the stupid thing he just said to a dying man.

Tim nodded. "Right, I'm trying for the same outcome." He gave Ray a big smile. "We seem to be thinking the same way. And Alyson should sing her butt off and enjoy."

Tim leaned forward offering his hand to Ray, Ray

took hold.

"You're right, Alyson should sing her head off and enjoy," echoed Ray.

Chapter Twenty-Nine

Wendy felt so good about the fact that her ladies were gung ho with the prospect of becoming entertainers. They were there for her, rehearsals two afternoons a week and the one evening over the weekend as planned, very seldom did they miss any. She now had them understanding how to read sheet music up to a point. They enjoyed practising and understanding synchronisation, hand and body movement giving out a musical language with rhythm to the music they sang. They excelled when they sang 'Autumn Leaves', and 'Moon River'. It was hard and demanding for her but she was in her glory, she loved every moment of it. Louise's keyboard had virtually become redundant but for the time' Wendy needed to demonstrate an effect. But Louise was still part of the team and always ready to turn her hand to any job. Now it was evening as she sat in Dot Roberts's sitting room which had become Dot's workroom. There was a sewing machine on the table at the window, and two tailor's dummies partly dressed in long gowns. Wendy sat in the armchair between the two tailor's dummies and watched the proceedings. Arlene stood on the footstool wearing a red evening dress with a black sash as Dot pinned up the bottom hem. Wendy, Jan and Emily in a mixture of evening gowns waited their turn on the footstool and the final adjustments to their gowns.

Arlene looked back over her shoulder at Wendy. "£7,300!" she said loudly.

"I shouldn't have said anything," Wendy replied.

"Yes you should, she's our friend as well," answered Arlene adamantly.

Emily nodded. "I thought my old mum had problems when my dad died, like £2,000, but £7,300, that's a lot of money!"

The doorbell rang, and Jan got to her feet. "I'll get it." she raised her too-long gown from the floor and made her way to the door. Moments later she was back with Lian. Lian carried a black evening gown over her arm.

Wendy smiled. "That's a nice dress, Lian."

Lian beamed. "Thanks."

Dot got to her feet from pinning Arlene's dress. "Right, next."

Arlene stepped off the footstool and Jan took her

place. Dot again dropped to her knees and started to pin the hem of Jan's gown.

"We've been talking about Alyson and how we could help her," said Wendy.

Lian sat on the sofa. "I help some."

"We all will," answered Jan from the footstool.

Wendy nodded. "If we all put something into the hat it's going to help."

Dot looked up from her pinning. "It's a big chunk of money; we need a way to raise it for them."

"I have an idea," mused Arlene. "We have a good set of songs we can perform, let's put on our first show in Bedfordshire at the senior centre, club for the assisted living centre and any other place that will take us. Say £5 a ticket for charity."

"It'll all add up," said Jan. "Do you think we are ready, maestro?"

It only took a moment of thought from Wendy. "I know you are . . . I think that's a good idea," she added with enthusiasm.

Dot, with a mouth full of pins, yelled an almost distinguishable, "*Good.*"

"We have songs we are happy with," Wendy

exclaimed. "That should give us maybe sixteen, maybe twenty, minutes of entertainment."

"We could ask for donations," said Jan. "That way we may get more than £5!"

"Donations for what?" Wendy frowned.

"Tim," said Dot, emptying her mouth of pins.

Wendy shook her head. "I *don't* think so. I'm doubtful . . . Alyson *may* go along with it. For sure Tim won't, he's a proud man – I think we stick to it just being a charity."

"Right," agreed Jan after a moment of thought. "We know which charity it is . . . The audience doesn't need to know."

"Right, we know," said Lian.

Wendy's brain was racing. "If we are doing it for charity I think we may be able to get a booking fee, plus donations."

"How?" asked Jan.

"Woburn Golf Club is having its annual dinner and dance at the Bedford Arms next weekend," said Wendy. Ray's a member, and so are Dot, Kay and Arlene's husbands. Also, Louise's Paul is the club secretary and treasurer!"

Jan stepped off the footstool and an eager Lian climbed on. Wendy fished out her mobile phone and dialled a number; she got her connection. "Louise, it's Wendy, I need to talk with you."

Chapter Thirty

Wendy was lucky, her little Smart Car beat the young guy's Volvo into a parking spot directly opposite Bellwood Electronics. She parked and she and Louise climbed out. Wendy locked the car and they made their way across the road to Bellwood's electronic shop, dodging the Ampthill stream of traffic. Bellwood Electronics was Paul and Louise's pride and joy. It used to be a greengrocer's shop and was set between Cheeseman's the chemist and the Post Office. Now instead of vegetables adorning the front window, there was a keyboard very much like the one Louise used, plus Wi-Fi equipment, DVD players, and other pieces of electronic equipment to tempt the onlookers.

Louise held the door open for Wendy, closing it after her. The inside of the shop was just as tempting as the view through the window. The shelves and stands displayed amplifiers, Hi-Fi equipment, Blu-ray, CD players, and other electronics. On the back wall were a home theatre and audio entertainment system, set up in front of a black leather sofa.

Linda, a young attractive blonde girl, sat behind the counter and worked on a computer. She stopped typing and looked up with a smile at Louise and Wendy. "Hi, Louise."

"Hi, Linda. This is Mrs Knight . . . He knows we're coming in," she said, pointing to the closed door.

Linda nodded, stood, and went to the alcove door. "Paul," she called, "your wife's here." She moved back behind the counter.

Paul popped his head out from the alcove. "Hello, you two, sit yourselves down. Would you like some coffee?" They both declined. He motioned them to the sofa in front of the home entertainment display. Taking a stool he sat and faced them. "Louise told me about Tim and Alyson, sorry to hear they're having such a bad time."

Wendy nodded. "Bad doesn't even get close, Paul – Tim will be lucky to be around for Christmas!"

Louise gasped. "Wendy, you never told us that."

Wendy sighed. "I know . . . it's not something Alyson would want me broadcasting. So please forget I said it."

Louise looked at Paul. "I told Wendy we'll do what we can to help."

Wendy looked from one to the other. "That's super of

you both."

Paul agreed with a nod. "I talked with the club committee this morning and I can officially book your act at £300, as it is for a charity event."

Louise leaned over to him and kissed him on the cheek. "That's wonderful, sweetheart."

Wendy scratched her head and frowned. "We're worried about collecting money in the name of charity and then giving it to Alyson and Tim."

"Don't worry," answered Louise. "It would be classed as a charitable act and all above board. Your giving has a charity purpose, right, Paul?"

Paul agreed. "Right, but I don't think that's going to be your biggest problem," he said thoughtfully, looking from one to the other.

Wendy frowned. "What do you mean?"

"Well, you're an acapella musical group of seven ladies . . . That's fine when you have a captive audience sitting in chairs, in an auditorium, senior centre, a place where they've come to sit and listen to you sing. No, you're going to be entertaining at the Golf Club's dinner and dance. *Dance*! You can't dance to acapella, it just doesn't go together."

Wendy and Louise looked at each other, knowing he was right. To dance, you need a beat and a stronger and louder tempo. Wendy's original plan was never to book them for a dinner and dance. She was only interested in them singing to entertain, not to dance to. So they didn't become chocolate teapots.

Louise looked at Wendy. "Now I'm worried. Seven girls and me at a lone piano, would not sound too good . . . could kill the act before it even gets started!"

Louise and Wendy looked at Paul! "Don't panic, and I hope you don't mind but, I knew you were going to have this problem, so Johnny Royal's our dance band for the evening. I told him what you girls had in mind and you were doing it for charity. He'll work with you in setting something up."

"Mind?" said Wendy. "Is it alright if I fall in love with him?"

They laughed. Paul went over to Linda at the counter and asked her something. She wrote something on a piece of paper and handed it to Paul, and he passed it on to Wendy.

"This is Johnny's number; you need to talk to him he has some ideas to put to you," said Paul.

Louise kissed Paul. "Dinner in bed tonight?"

"*Louise!*" exclaimed Wendy.

Chapter Thirty-One

Arlene, Jan, Kay, Lian and Emily were all seated at their table in the window seat of the Chequers. Kelly was behind the bar chatting with a few customers. The pub was not that busy this lunchtime.

"Is anyone else as nervous as I am about actually singing in public?" asked Jan.

Emily giggled. "I have never done anything like it in my life!"

The door swung open and Wendy burst through. Kay who faced the door spotted her. "She's here," she said. All heads turned to the door and Wendy.

Before Wendy was halfway across the room she hollered, "Kelly, greetings, G&T's and another round for the sexy sixties." Wendy moved to the table and her waiting chair. She continued, "Alyson couldn't make it, she's working, and Louise is working on something for the act."

"What's with the sexy sixties?" asked Arlene hesitantly.

"I thought that's a good name for our group, what do

you think?" asked Wendy.

"Yuck," said Jan as she mimed fingers going down her throat.

"That is terrible, and *so* not us," exclaimed Emily.

Arlene laughed. "Speak for yourself."

Everyone laughed as Kelly brought over their drinks.

"Not nice. Not us, we, not sex, we songbirds," said Lian.

All eyes went to Lian. Lian looked from one to the other with uneasiness. "What I say . . . What's wrong?"

Wendy smiled. "You just, named us, The Songbirds."

They all beamed and nodded in agreement, but for Lian Meng. Then in unison, "*The Songbirds*."

Jan pointed at Wendy. "You found us and you're putting us together, so we are "'Wendy Knight and The Songbirds'."

All agreed, and so Wendy Knight and The Songbirds were born.

Chapter Thirty-Two

The glass illuminated the announcement case that was mounted on the entrance steps to the Bedford Arms Hotel in Woburn. It read.

'Woburn Golf Club Dinner & Dance
To The Music Of Johnny Royal And His Band
Also Featuring A Charity Performance
By Wendy Knight And The Songbirds.'

There was a chill in the air as a sprinkling of late arrivals climbed the steps and disappeared into the lobby of the hotel.

* * *

Johnny Royal's band played while Johnny performed the vocal to 'That Old Black Magic.' It was a good turnout, with around sixty people enjoying the black-tie event. At the moment most were on the dancefloor dancing to the music, as others munched on pre-dinner canapés and drinks and mingled with friends. Waiters, dressed in black pants, white shirts, and black bowties, flitted around with drinks and finger food. The waitresses wore white blouses and black skirts. Thirty tables surrounded the dance floor, some guests were already seated at their tables, and others table-hopped and exchanged pleasantries. On each side of the room, adjacent to the band, were ceiling-to-floor red curtains, the one on the left concealed the huddled Songbirds in beautifully created gowns by Dot. Louise was putting the finishing touches to the concealed radio microphones hidden in the Songbirds' hair, the microphone barely protruding from the edge of their hairline, hardly noticeable when it was dabbed with the same tone make-up the ladies wore.

"I never knew there was such a thing as hairline microphones," said Emily as Louise fiddled to get hers just right. "I thought they were all like the one we have on a stick."

Louise made the final adjustment. "These are top-notch microphones, Emily, they're *radio* microphones: no wire so you can move around wherever you want. Paul rented them, especially for us."

"In the hair is best for a clear signal," added Wendy. "The only thing you have to remember is when they are turned on you are live and whatever you say can be heard, not just when you sing."

"I am so nervous," said Arlene.

Lian slipped her arm through Arlene's. "You be good."

"I know how she feels!" exclaimed Jan.

"Ditto," replied Kay.

"We so be good, you see," said Lian.

"Right," murmured Wendy holding her hand up for the high-five. "Yes, we are. All for one and one for all."

They all responded with a high-five to each other as 'That Old Black Magic' came to an end, and applause filled the ballroom.

"Now listen up," hollered Wendy above the applause from the ballroom. "Your mics will go *live* from the moment Johnny gives count into our first number 'As Time Goes By', so no talking after that, *right*, remember your microphones will be live . . . here we go, you four. Goodbye and break a leg."

With that, Arlene, Kay, Lian and Emily headed out beyond the curtains to their tables.

Lian grabbed Emily's arm. *"Break my leg?"* asked a puzzled Lian.

Emily giggled. "It's complicated. I'll explain later."

* * *

'That Old Black Magic' had been Johnny Royal's fifth

vocal of the evening, and he was ready for a break. As the applause died, he acknowledged his thanks to the audience and dancers as they left the dance floor and returned to their tables. He took the microphone from its stand and moved down onto the dance floor, distancing himself from the orchestra. "Ladies and Gentlemen," he announced *twice*. After a pause, the guests took notice. "Ladies and Gentlemen." Johnny waved his hand in the air. "Thank you, thank you, everyone . . . Are we having a good time?" Loud cheers of *yes* and *great*, went up from around the ballroom. Johnny quieted them once again with a wave. "Ladies and gentlemen your attention, *please*. We now have a treat for you . . . The premier performance of a group of young ladies, Wendy Knight, and The Songbirds." Applause erupted from the crowd plus whistles and shouts all around. "The Songbirds are here tonight not only to entertain you, but they are also singing on behalf of a charity and to raise a little money. *So*, remember that, when you're listening to their dulcet tones, and give your support with a donation in the envelopes placed on your tables . . . Now, without more ado, I have the pleasure of presenting Wendy Knight and The Songbirds."

Applause echoed around the room and the lights dimmed as Wendy, Jan and Alyson emerged from behind the curtain moving to the three microphones in front of the orchestra. Wendy stepped behind the centre microphone, Jan the one on her left, Alyson on the right. Spotlights from above came on illuminating the three ladies dressed to perfection in Dot's creations. The other Songbirds sat in the dimly lit room at different tables near the stage. Arlene sat between Ray and Ken, who had been warned not to talk to her because of the radio microphones. Across from them sat Kevan, Johanna and Rebecca. Kay was at a table for four next to Gary and Dot, again all had been told about the microphones. Lian was next to Harry at a ten table and Emily with Brian at another four table.

Wendy was at home behind the microphone and in front of an orchestra, she nodded to Johnny. Johnny gave a count into 'As Time Goes By'. Wendy, Jan and Alyson, with the orchestra, hummed the intro with harmonisation. Wendy sang the first verse.

It was Jan's turn to sing and she did, a touch shaky on the first line but then she found her comfort zone. Alyson now harmonised with Wendy.

To Ken's surprise, and everyone else at the table, a spotlight came to life above their table and Arlene stood and positioned herself behind Ken, her hands on his shoulders. The same thing happened at Lian, Kay and Emily's tables in turn.

Arlene sang nervously at first.

Then it was Kay's turn, a touch too soft but it built.

Lian was more than ready.

The orchestra took the middle eight as Arlene, Kay, Lian and Emily glided regally across the dance floor in their evening gowns to join Wendy, Alyson and Jan. Arlene and Kay lined up between Jan and Wendy, Lian and Emily between Wendy and Alyson. All the Songbirds were now in a row as Johnny led the orchestra back in and they sang as one.

Applause all around, plus vigorous applause from the family. The Songbirds' husbands were on their feet and were very proud men. Ray clapped his hands so hard they began to sting.

Wendy and The Songbirds were overwhelmed with the response to their performance, they joined hands and bowed three times in appreciation. As the room settled down Johnny Royal struck up the orchestra with

'Sugarbush'. The Songbirds' radio microphones were now turned off, they went three to a microphone to each side of Wendy's centre microphone. They sang with all their hearts . . . And sang with confidence as the dancers swirled around in front of them.

'Sugarbush' segued into, 'You Make Me Feel So Young', then 'Let Yourself Go' and on and on through their prepared and agreed list of songs. The Songbirds were well and truly launched, especially at the Bedford Arms.

Chapter Thirty-Three

Happy Songbirds Wendy, Arlene, Jan, Lian, Kay, Dot and Emily sat around Robert's dining table. Jan placed the last £5 note on the money stack alongside the cheques. All were set out neatly on the table in front of them. Jan looked up and smiled at The Songbirds saying, "With the £300 fee from the Golf Club and £275 from donations we have . . ."

" . . . £575," said Kay, "though not enough to ease the pain and worry I fear."

"No," agreed Arlene.

"Is Alyson at work?" asked Emily.

Wendy nodded.

"Has she any idea we are doing it for her and Tim?" asked Kay.

Wendy shook her head. "No – and I have yet to work out how I'm going to give it to her."

Emily sighed, "£575 from £7,300."

"£6,725," calculated Kay.

Arlene looked around at the sad faces. "Hey come on, you lot, we did our best. Every little is going to help. We do some more shows and it's going to add up."

Lian sat upright in her chair and slapped the tabletop. "We do contress for £2,500."

Wendy looked at her confused as did the others. "Contress! What the hell is contress?" Wendy asked.

"Us, sing contress, Palace Theatre," said Lian frustrated.

Phil, carrying an open newspaper, entered from the hall. "She means contest." He had been listening from the kitchen. "Hello, Mrs Meng."

She waved to him.

Phil placed the paper on the table in front of Wendy. "It's here in the paper. Palace Theatre's amateur talent contest in Bedford. First prize £2,500, the second £1,500 and the third £500."

Wendy looked at the paper. "*Contest!* You mean contest."

"Yes contress," said Lian with a smile. "We sing."

Phil laughed. "She right, contress, listen to the lady." He returned to the kitchen smiling from ear to ear.

"It's not £6,725, but it would go a long way to help, whether it's first, second or third!" exclaimed Wendy.

They looked from one to another in turn; smiles crept

onto their faces.

Jan, who sat next to Lian, hugged her. "Good one, Lian, looks as if we are going to the contress."

Wendy nodded. "Jan's right . . . Good one, Lian."

All agreed.

Chapter Thirty-Four

The marquee outside the Palace Theatre displayed the up-and-coming amateur talent show. Wendy, holding a bundle of programmes and with Ray in tow, exited the theatre and joined the waiting Songbirds, Arlene, Kay, Emily, Louise, and Lian. Wendy read the programme out loud to the waiting Songbirds, "Wendy Knight and The Songbirds, third on the bill."

"*Really*," said Jan, sceptical.

"Really," echoed Wendy.

"Great," said Louise and punched the air.

Wendy laughed. "Right do we go for a drink to celebrate?" she asked.

Excited, they all voted for a celebratory drink. As they headed for their cars, Wendy hollered, "See, you're all excited now. You all thought we were past it when we started The Songbirds months ago."

Emily giggled. "That's show business for you."

Wendy smiled at her. "Funny . . . See you at the Chequers."

Chapter Thirty-Five

Wendy drove the Smart Car into their drive and up to the garage door. Ray climbed out and opened the hatchback. Wendy joined him as he lifted out the carrier bag and she gathered up the bundle of theatre programmes. "That everything?" Ray asked.

"Yep," she replied and closed the hatchback. Ray, with the carrier bag, headed for the house and unlocked the front door, disappearing inside.

"*Wendy.*" She turned on hearing her name called. It was Alyson, getting out of her car at their drive's entrance. Wendy managed to wave without dropping the programmes and walked down the drive to meet her. She could see by Alyson's expression that all was not well! "Something wrong?" she asked concerned.

Ray watched them from the sitting room window, he shook his head and thought, *tears at bedtime.*

Alyson took an envelope from her pocket. She held the envelope inches from Wendy's face. "What do you know about this?"

"*Me?*" was Wendy's lame response.

"Yes . . .*You.*" She waved the envelope back and forth. "There's £1,075 in here, and You put it through our letterbox."

It seldom happened that Wendy was lost for words . . . but now she was. She exhaled and looked up to the heavens, *this* was one of those times. Wendy lowered her head and looked at Alyson. "Alyson." She looped her arm through Alyson's, turned her around, and walked her back toward her car. "You're right, £500 came from Ray and me," she admitted. "The other from our show, the fee, and donations."

They came to a stop at the car, and Alyson turned to Wendy. "Wendy, I don't wanna seem ungrateful, but we can't take it."

Wendy placed her hands on Alyson's shoulder. "Now you listen to me. If Ray and I couldn't afford it, you wouldn't have it there in that envelope. All of us wanted to do it for you and Tim. All of us are determined to get rid of this debt of yours. If we'd known how to pay the bills without you knowing we would have."

"But, Wendy, don't you understand?. . We can't pay you back."

"Are you deaf?" Wendy exclaimed. "We don't need it

. . . don't want it paid back. So, please don't be too proud to take help when your friends want to help."

Alyson's eyes brimmed with tears, and she looked at the envelope still in her hand. "Wendy, I have to tell you, it's a Godsend."

Wendy opened the car door, and Alyson slid in behind the wheel. "I may as well tell you now that you're going to have to swallow your pride again soon. Now listen, this is strictly entre nous. That's French, for between us."

Alyson looked up at her from behind the wheel. "I know what it means!" She reached out and took Wendy's hand in hers. "This is all tied up with Ray's visit with Tim right?"

"No, not really, but he was concerned like we all were when we found out things were not going well for you both."

Ray still watched from the window. He breathed a sigh of relief knowing the two friends had sorted out their problem. *No tears at bedtime.*

At the car, Wendy leaned closer to Alyson. "Now, about this talent competition . . ."

Alyson turned to her. " . . . What talent competition?"

Chapter Thirty-Six

Ray watched a rerun of *Foyle's War* propped up in bed nice and cosy as Wendy edged her way through the door with their nightly mug of hot chocolate in each hand. She handed him his mug and went around to her side of the bed and put her mug on the nightstand, next to the stack of Bedford Palace programmes, then climbed into bed. She picked up her mug and a programme from the stack and thumbed through it as she sipped the hot chocolate. She reached the centre page. "We are third on the bill," she said.

Ray watched the television. "I know . . . You've told me a few times now."

Wendy nodded. "Number one is Peppy Nutter, the New Age Rapper . . . Number two damn it!"

"What?" said Ray hitting the pause button on *Foyle's War*.

"Number two are The Tapping Toddlers," she exclaimed. "Never act with children or animals, they'll steal the show."

"They may not be that good," Ray tried to

reassure her.

Wendy smiled, leaned over, and kissed him on the cheek. She went back to the programme saying, "I love you, Ray Knight . . . *Oh my God*," she yelled stopping him from returning to *Foyle's War*.

"What now?" he asked.

Wendy sat bolt upright, splashing her chocolate over the top of the mug. "*Accompaniment*! We don't have accompaniment, we don't have music. We are acapella."

"You have a CD," said Ray.

Wendy shook her head. "Not allowed. Has to be live. God, I'm an idiot." She sat silent for a moment, her thoughts racing.

Ray turned to her. "Johnny Royal did you a favour last time; see if he'll come through again."

She shook her head. "Even if he would, he can't. He's a professional dance band. You need to be an amateur, It's an amateur talent show."

"That's stupid, it's a talent competition and you're talent. You're a group of singers. You sing. You make music!"

"You know that . . . I know that, but the word music is synonymous with instruments brass, violins, drums, pianos, trumpets . . . whatever," moaned Wendy.

"You have Louise with her keyboard."

Wendy shook her head. "She'll be lost against our voices."

Ray's hackles were now up. "I still say it's stupid."

"I hear what you're saying, but it's here in black and white, quote, live accompaniment."

Again Ray shook his head. "But you're an act that doesn't need it." Ray spotted the chocolate on the duvet. "You've spilt chocolate on the bed cover."

Wendy looked at him with a blank stare. "I'm not taking any chances of being disqualified before we even start. What time is it?"

Ray looked at the clock on his nightstand. "Just after 9:00. Did you hear what I said? there is chocolate on the . . .!"

" . . . I know, I'll fix it." Wendy climbed out of bed, grabbed the cordless phone and punched in a number.

"Who are you calling?" Ray snapped.

Wendy headed for the door. "A number I know by heart," she called back to him. "Hello, London Palladium?" he heard her say as she disappeared into the hall and down the stairs.

Ray strained to listen to her fading voice. He gave up on *Foyle's War* and turned off the television, took off his watch and placed it on the nightstand, picked up his book, and prepared to read. Before he had a chance to open the book Wendy scurried back into the room, damp cloth in one hand, phone to her ear with the other.

"That's great," she said into the phone. "Please, thank everyone from me." She cradled the phone and started work with the damp cloth on the chocolate stain. She succeeded to her satisfaction: the duvet cover was wet but chocolate-free. She climbed back into bed.

"So!" exclaimed Ray. "What was that all about?"

"You'll see – I hope!" She turned off her light and snuggled up close to Ray. "Turn off the light."

"I was reading!" he said.

She reached over and turned off his light. There was silence in the darkness. She heard him put his book down, again quiet prevailed until Wendy said softly, "You sleepy?"

"No," he replied faintly.

"Good," she whispered.

Chapter Thirty-Seven

"You're all very good, Gran," said Rebecca seated next to Wendy in the Smart Car as they drove down the hill out of Millbrook.

Wendy nodded. "They have all worked their socks off over the last weeks."

"I know," agreed Rebecca. "*And* at their age."

"Hey watch it," laughed Wendy. "They're my age . . . So don't go there, young Rebecca."

"Sorry, Gran."

"So you should be. You're young, your whole life is in front of you."

"I said I'm sorry."

"I know you are." Wendy smiled. Silence hung for a moment, Wendy broke it. "It's alright, Rebecca. I understand. I've been there and got the worn-out T-shirt."

Rebecca laughed.

"Let me remind you of one thing, then I'll say no more, right?" said Wendy as she gave Rebecca a sideways glance.

"Right," echoed Rebecca.

"What goes around comes around. We all have to die, and we all get old if we're lucky. Even you young ones who call us wrinklies."

"Gran, you're depressing me."

"Oh, why's that?"

Rebecca looked at her granny sheepishly. "Because I love you and I don't want you ever to die."

Wendy reached over and hugged her.

Rebecca turned to Wendy, her eyes lit up. "I've got you a fan club together from school. We're going to be at the show to give support," she said with excitement.

"That's wonderful. We're certainly going to need it."

"What are you going to be wearing?"

"Louise got us sponsorship from Marks and Sparks. We have seven matching blouses and skirts. Dot is doing alterations."

"You're going to look wonderful, I know it."

Wendy smiled listening to probably her biggest fan.

Chapter Thirty-Eight

Ray, Phil, and Brian, in work clothes, stood together looking at their handiwork.

"What do you think?" asked Brian . . . his question had little confidence.

"I think it looks good," answered Ray. "They're going to love it."

Phil nodded. "I like it."

Brian nodded. "There's only one way to find out!"

Chapter Thirty-Nine

In the barn's rehearsal space, the full complement of glum-faced Songbirds banded together: Arlene, Jan, Kay, Emily, Alyson and Lian all in sweats. Wendy faced them. "Well, I'm here, what's the problem?"

"We need to talk," announced Arlene.

"I don't like the sound of this," Wendy said as The Songbirds gathered around and found seats.

Arlene twice cleared her throat, and after a moment she found her voice with hesitancy. "Well . . . we've all been talking and find we are of one mind – *terrified.*"

All agreed with groans and nods.

Wendy looked at them puzzled. "Terrified of what?"

Arlene spread her palms to the heavens. "Of going on stage, that terrified. Out there in front of hundreds of people, big terrified!"

Wendy frowned.

"It's alright for you," said Kay. "You and Alyson, you know show business. You two have sung in front of hundreds of people."

"Wendy," said Jan, "you have been on stage all your

life. I for one have never been on a stage."

Wendy gave them a big smile. "What about the other night? You all did so well."

"That was different," said Emily. "Fifty people and between us we knew every one of them."

Again there was an all-around agreement.

Wendy looked at them in turn and nodded. "I'm an idiot, they're right," she said looking at Alyson. "I've charged ahead without thinking . . . I'm sorry."

"We do not say we'll not do it," said Lian. "But understand, scary. You teach us to suck it up and get out there!"

Wendy nodded with a smile. "That's a class I've never taught, but . . ."

Alyson burst into tears. " . . . It's my fault. You're all doing this to help Tim and me . . ."

" . . . Alyson, zip it. If we do this we're going to be doing it because we want to, as well as help you and Tim. You know why I started us off on this. I'm tired of people thinking sixty-five, seventy is the end, that we are in the dead zone! Well we're not, we still have lots to offer."

All agreed. Alyson nodded and shrugged feeling embarrassed.

Wendy looked at The Songbirds. "I understand, I do, but you see . . . When that curtain goes up the fear will go with it. The footlights will hit you in the face and the applause will make your heart pound . . . trust me."

"Shut up, Wendy, You're frightening me more. Footlights, applause," said Arlene.

"What we forget the words?" asked Lian.

"That could be big trouble for you, Lian," answered Wendy. "If you do, we won't buy your takeaway ever again."

Lian thought for a moment then cracked a smile. "I no forget words." Lian had put everything right, and everyone smiled.

Wendy turned to Alyson. "Alyson, you're one of our best singers, are you afraid?"

"Yes," replied Alyson.

"*Alyson*," exclaimed Wendy, "you are supposed to agree with me!" Wendy looked around at the smiling faces. "I know it's scary, I also know you can do it, we all can."

At that point, the door opened and Brian stood there. "Ladies, come with me please, I have something to show you."

The Songbirds, with looks back and forth, obeyed, got to their feet and murmured. Their curiosity aroused, they followed Brian out of the barn.

* * *

Led by Brian, the procession of Songbirds snaked their way between the two buildings and arrived at the door of his workshop. Brian opened the door and stood aside as The Songbirds filed past him. Once in the workshop, they stood amazed at what confronted them. Wendy made her way to the front. They were all looking at a ten-by-eight stage backdrop, cut out of plywood and beautifully painted. It depicted shrubbery and flowers. In turn, the shrubbery was covered in cut-outs of small songbirds amongst the flowers and leaves.

Emily turned to her husband. "Brian, my darling wonderful man." And she hugged him, as The Songbirds applauded.

Brian held his hands up, the applause stopped and Brian pointed toward the backdrop. "Gentlemen, take a bow." And from behind the scenic backdrop stepped Ray and Phil, they took a bow. Again the ladies applauded.

Wendy clapped her hands repeatedly. She was so happy. "This is where you've been hiding! I thought you'd got a girlfriend." She hugged him. "It's great." She hugged Phil and then clapped Brian on the back. Everyone followed suit. Wendy stood aside with Ray and watched the excitement shared by all. The backdrop was a hit.

One by one, they all sensed Wendy watching them. The merriment died down and Wendy stood, her arm linked to Ray's. She nodded and smiled. *"Terrified*! – Well, are we going to let The Songbirds go to waste?" she shouted.

The Songbirds looked at each other, and then as one voice shouted back, "*No*."

Chapter Forty

In front of the Palace Theatre, Rebecca and five of her school pals handed out leaflets and sang the praises of The Songbirds to patrons of the night's entertainment.

* * *

While backstage of the Palace was a hive of activity. Contestants and theatre crew moved back and forth between the curtains and backdrops making ready. Ray, Dot and Phil came through the stage door carrying The Songbirds' dresses. They headed down the stairs to the dressing rooms.

* * *

The Songbirds had been allocated the biggest dressing room, known as the chorus dressing room, because of their numbers *and* consideration of their age. Wendy was fit to be tied when the age bit was announced. It took Alyson and Kay five minutes to calm her down. The Songbirds, in their robes, were seated in front of the mirror that covered the back wall of the room, all working on their make-up. Wendy and Arlene were shoulder to shoulder at the far end of the room and their portion of the mirror. Jan and Kay worked on their hair. Emily and Louise fixed Alyson and Lian's radio microphones in their hairlines. Ray, Dot, and Phil entered with the dresses.

Wendy spotted them and called out, "Everyone okay?"

There was agreement all around as Dot handed out their dresses.

"I have to go check on our backdrop," yelled Ray. He did an about-turn followed by Phil and they were gone. Dot laid out the dresses on the centre table.

Arlene looked at Wendy's reflection in the mirror. She turned and nudged Jan who sat to her right working on her eyelashes. She motioned Jan to look at Wendy's reflection in the mirror.

Jan glanced at Wendy through the mirror. "That's one heck of a lot of make-up," she said as she looked at Wendy's reflection.

The others took notice and gathered around to view Wendy's make-up.

Wendy looked back at their reflections lined up behind her. "Sorry, ladies, I never covered this part of show business. On stage, more is better. If you want them to see your good looks you have to point them out . . . More is better." She gave a final swipe of lip gloss to her lower lip.

Everyone was back to their chairs in a flash, muttering, "More is better."

There was a knock at the door followed by Ray shouting, "Are you ladies respectable?"

Wendy hollered, "Yes, we're all married." Everyone laughed. "Come in, Ray," Wendy called.

Ray came in with Phil and the Stage Manager, Terri, a short round plump lady in her thirties, she was as sharp as a tack, but hell on wheels according to everybody who knew her. Terri wore a headset with a microphone attached. "Everyone, this is Terri the Stage Manager," Ray announced.

Terri cast her eye over the musical group, then. "Terri it is," she said firmly. "Or, commonly known backstage as *God*. Don't let the agenda worry you I am God as you will learn."

Phil cracked a smile and mimicked shuddering as he started to hang the dresses on hangers as Dot handed them to him.

The Songbirds, intimidated by the presence of Terri, continued with their make-up.

Terri shouted, "*Hello*." And in unison, she had their attention. All swung around in their chairs and faced her, this included Ray, Phil, Dot and Louise who stood behind her, back to the door. Terri continued very loudly so that at a later date no one could claim they had not heard her. "Now listen up, God is talking. I will give you your call to stage with warnings at ten minutes, eight, and six intervals. On six I want your backsides standing by in the wings. Understood?"

The Songbirds looked from one to another in silence, mouths open.

Again Terri continued. "*Understood*?" she shouted.

As one voice, military-style, they yelled, "*Yes, God*."

Terri turned for the door but had second thoughts. Her demeanour changed. She lowered her voice and with a smile, she said, "Break a leg, ladies. Have fun." And with that, she was gone, hiding a smile.

"Wow," said Wendy. "I've had some stage managers in my time, but God here beats the lot."

The door burst open and Terri now pushed in Henry and three other men, Tony, Blake and Sam, all of the same age range as Henry. Terri hollered, "Your backup players. We don't have any more dressing rooms. Enjoy."

"But we have to change," protested Emily.

Terri laughed. "Wake up, girl, this is show business." Terri stepped out once again, slamming the door behind her.

Wendy looked at Ray. She knew she was on the spot! *Change of subject.* "Scenery," she announced. "Okay, Ray!"

"Forget the scenery," said Kay. "How come we have backup *and* we're sharing dressing rooms?"

Wendy took a breath. "This was my surprise for you, The Harmonicas." She patted Henry on his back. "Henry here is a very old friend from my Palladium days. He and his buddies are our music men."

"Harmonicas?" questioned Jan. She turned to Henry. "No offence."

"None taken." Henry smiled. He looked at Wendy and shrugged. "We need to change into our tuxes."

"There are the men's toilets," smiled Alyson.

Wendy looked at Henry and raised an eyebrow. "Do you mind?"

Henry chuckled and shook his head. "That's show business." He beckoned to The Harmonicas and they followed him through the door to find the toilets.

Wendy started to change, feeling guilty about turfing Henry and his buddies out. "That was a bit mean of us," she voiced.

Arlene nailed her with an icy look. "Not us. You . . . You never said a word about The Harmonicas. You *never* said a word about us having backing until yesterday when you told us about the contest rules, we thought it was going to be Louise."

Wendy looked around at the questioning faces of The Songbirds all staring at her and nodded. "You're right," she muttered.

"What was that?" asked Dot.

"I said you're right," agreed Wendy speaking louder.

"You never said it, you muttered it," added Dot.

"Point taken," Wendy murmured heading for her dress on the rack and shouting, "*You're right*!"

Emily, at Wendy's side, took her dress from the rack. "Wendy, if they are our band, shouldn't we have rehearsed with them?"

By now Wendy had got her act together and back in charge. "Believe me, Henry and the boys will do fine."

"I hope so," giggled Emily. "I thought I had butterflies

in my tummy before, now I have jet planes flying around."

The PA system over the mirror came to life startling everyone. Terri's voice calmly announced, '*Peppy Nutter . . . ten minutes please.*' Ray and Phil were physically shoved out as everyone made for their costumes.

* * *

Backstage was a hive of activity. Offstage, Ray and Phil made last-minute adjustments to The Songbirds' backdrop as Terri's not-quite-so-calm voice came over the speaker, '*Nutter, eight minutes.*' In the wings, Henry and The Harmonicas connected radio microphones to their harmonicas, which in turn would feed the amplifiers. Terri's voice came to life again, this time with an edge to it. '*Nutter, six minutes to stage.*'

* * *

Peppy Nutter was a young, confident man, around eighteen, wearing jeans, with the crotch almost down to his ankles. The rest of his ensemble was a Hawaiian shirt and baseball cap askew. He was accompanied by his bongo player, bongo drum under his arm again in his teens, and dressed in the same loud style as Peppy. They hurried to Terri's side in the wings. From the stage came the voice of the compere overflowing with bubbling charisma. '*Ladies and gentlemen, a big welcome for the rapper to beat all rappers . . . Peppy Nutter.*' The audience's applause reverberated backstage as Terri mercilessly pushed Peppy Nutter onto the stage, the bongo player at his heels. Peppy and the bongo player moved to the centre of the stage against a psychedelic backdrop. Immediately the bongo player started a beat, and Peppy was rapping, his talk conversation of rhythm, with mostly rhyming patter. By the sound of the audience following along with rhythmic hand clapping they seemed to be enjoying Peppy Nutter and his rap

* * *

In the audience, Johanna, Kevan, Rebecca and her school friends' heads bobbed from side to side with the beat. Two rows back were the husbands, Ken, Frank, Brian, and Gary. To the side in the small disabled section was Sue with her father Tim in his wheelchair. Sadly Tim needed to be attached to his oxygen cylinder, but he certainly seemed to be enjoying himself. All seemed to like Peppy Nutter's rap, although not understanding much of it, the beat was contagious. The audience liked him by the way their heads were bobbing back and forth, up and down to the bongo rhythm.

Peppy was now high on his lyrics.

'I am here cos I wanna be seen

You'll know when I'm coming you'll know when I've been

I'm here to rap so I'm here to win if I don't get the prize it'll be a sin

My mother is sick and my father don't work

I keep telling him he's a total jerk.'

Terri stood in the wings, checking her watch. "Tapping Toddlers, ten minutes please," she announced calmly.

* * *

Back in the dressing room, The Songbirds put the finishing touches to their dresses and make-up. Terri's voice came through the speakers, not quite as calm as before. *'Tapping Toddlers, eight minutes.'* Then calmly, *'The Songbirds, ten minutes, please.'* Excitement flowed over The Songbirds and they were ready. Terri's now sharp voice filled the room. *'Six minutes to stage, Toddlers.'* The Songbirds lined up at the door. Terri's voice again, this time not quite as calm. *'The Songbirds, eight minutes.'*

* * *

On stage, Peppy Nutter carried on rapping.

'*Wanna paint walls and wanna be hip.*

Want all the gear it's a total trip.

Wanna stay out with my friends all night.'

Terri and The Tapping Toddlers, ages six to eight, were at her side. All dressed neatly in red ruffled blouses and black pants.

Ray and Phil were close by as they balanced The Songbirds' backdrop between them.

Peppy was winding down.

'*Watch my movements watch me sing*

Vote me the winner if you get the chance

My sister's in rehab my brother's in jail

So have to keep rapping cos I don't wanna fail.'

There was moderate applause as Peppy and the bongo player exited the stage. The compere, a grey-haired man in his forties dressed in a tuxedo, moved on stage applauding the departed rapper. "Thank you, Peppy. Remember, you the audience have the vote. At the end of the show, we will bring out all competitors, and our applause meter. It will register the loudest applause given to each contestant. So . . . you the audience pick the winner. Right, next we have The Tapping Toddlers." The curtain opened to a backdrop of a ship with lollipops sticking out of its porthole and a grand piano to one side. Sitting at the piano, a dowdily-dressed woman, hands raised ready to strike the keys, which she did with much vigour. The introduction was 'On The Good Ship Lollipop'. From the wings, Terri directed The Tapping Toddlers on Stage. They entered the stage tapping and singing.

They were good, everyone loved to see children sing and dance and they had the audience from the go.

In the wings, Terri made a sharp announcement into her microphone. "Songbirds, on stage six minutes."

The Songbirds filed up the stairs to the wings and Terri, minus Dot and Louise.

Terri pointed to where they should stand. Then put her finger to her lips for quiet.

Ray and Phil stood by ready with the backdrop as, on stage, the children sang and tapped.

Wendy nudged Jan. "They sound good."

"Shush," hushed Terri.

Wendy forced a smile in Terri's direction, then whispered to Jan, "It was W.C. Fields who made the famous quote, '*Never work with children or animals, they will steal the show*'."

Terri leaned in closer and muttered, "And they will." Then not so calmly into her microphone, "The Bionics, six minutes."

The Tapping Toddlers took their bow to very good applause and danced off the stage past The Songbirds. All but Wendy smiled and waved to the children.

Wendy lowered her voice saying, "There goes the enemy . . . Don't say I never warned you!"

Lian tugged Wendy's arm. "They good."

Wendy looked daggers at her. "Shush."

Arlene and Alyson laughed.

From their side, Terri said, "For God's sake be quiet."

The curtain closed, and Ray and Phil rushed to put the backdrop in place. Terri beckoned to The Songbirds and they took up their places.

On stage Henry and the others were in place.

In front of the curtain, the compere took centre stage still applauding the toddlers. "Weren't they good?" he yelled, and the audience agreed with him. "Thank you The Tapping Toddlers." The audience settled. "Now we have a treat for you. Behind that curtain waiting to entertain are Wendy Knight and The Songbirds. *All* senior citizens totalling 454 years."

Johanna, Kevan, Rebecca and her friends cheered and whooped. Applause started up and the compere continued above the noise, mainly from The Songbirds' friends and family.

Then, through the amplifiers, the haunting sound of Henry's harmonica echoed the intro of 'You Belong To Me'. The theatre quietened. Henry played half tempo, then all The Harmonicas came in straight time picking up the intro. The curtain opened and The Songbirds took the stage.

In the audience, families and friends of The Songbirds and The Harmonicas looked on in awe. Tim with Sue at his side, both with tears in their eyes, looked up at The Songbirds, especially his wife Alyson. Their voices as smooth as velvet came in after the intro to 'You Belong To Me'.

They swayed to the music, hand and shoulder movement in perfect sync.

Their harmonisation was spot on. Wendy dared to look left and right at her Songbirds, truly they had come to fruition.

They reached the instrumental verse, The Songbirds hummed along playing the background to Henry and The Harmonicas. They sang back in with the last verse.

The music ended and applause erupted with lots of whooping and shouting. They had done it, this was not a row of chocolate teapots; they were The Songbirds, up and ready to go even though they were collecting their pensions. They took their bow and headed for the wings. The applause continued, and Terri signalled them to take another bow, which they did to more applause. From the wings Terri was now beckoning them off, they followed her signal and headed off stage.

* * *

In the wings, Terri shouted muted instructions to Ray and Phil. "Get your backdrop off my stage." They did as they were told. With much excitement and congratulations to each other, The Songbirds filed into what little space there was beyond the wings. Ray and Phil steadied the backdrop against the back wall then moved over to the girls, as did Henry and his buddies. There were more congratulations from everyone.

Behind them, Terri pushed the two Bionics dressed in leotards and carrying juggling skittles on stage. In the next breath, she was talking into the PA system sharply . . . "The Incredible George, six minutes." She turned to The Songbirds and used her hushed shout. "You lot, clear my stage." She looked at her watch. "For twenty-three minutes . . . Go!"

Wendy mimicked a shiver. "God has spoken." As one, they all headed for the stairwell.

Chapter Forty-One

The Songbirds filed back into the dressing room. Wendy had hardly managed to close the door when someone rapped on it. She did an about-turn and opened the door to an attractive, thirty-five-year-old blonde, flashing a big smile.

"Hello, I'm Jane . . . Jane Harris," she said with an even bigger smile. "BBC East, *Entertainment Tonight* show." She offered her hand.

There were mumbles around the room, '*BBC East, news, TV, Jane Harris*' and so on.

"We've been filming the show for the weekend's *Entertainment Tonight* show," Jane explained. "May we talk to you ladies for the segment?"

Wendy stepped aside. Jane and her videographer, a plain girl in her twenties, moved into the room.

"So, you total 454 years between you?" stated Jane without hesitation.

"Jane," said Wendy, "I don't know where those numbers came from . . . but do we have to go that route?"

"Yes," agreed Alyson, "why not talk about how

young we look."

There was agreement all around. Jane held her hands up in defence, laughing. "Okay, we can do that." She signalled the videographer to start filming.

* * *

Backstage The Songbirds' backdrop was being dismantled by Ray and Phil. Henry and his buddies packed up their speaker and amplifier, plus cables. On stage, Ken Baker, the country and western singer, performed 'Got A Little Country'.

Finished with the backdrop, Ray moved over to Henry. "Henry, thanks for coming down to help us out."

Henry nodded. "Anything for Wendy. She has a heart of gold, always did have. You're a lucky man."

Ray chuckled. "That's what she tells me."

Henry laughed.

Chapter Forty-Two

The master of ceremonies and compere of the show had explained to the audience that a clap-o-meter calculated the volume of applause given out by an audience for each act.

Within the next few minutes, Wendy and her Songbirds' name would be called and the machine would go to work calculating their score. All the acts had been brought back on stage for the judging by the device. They would be divided into two groups: stage right, losers, stage left, those still in the contest.

The compere, microphone in hand, continued to drum up excitement. Above him hung the giant monitor that displayed the clap-o-meter readings.

Wendy bit her lower lip as she looked along the line of losers to her right. So far, rapper, Peppy Nutter; the tumblers, The Bionics; a magician, The Incredible George; another singing group, The Carr Brothers; juggler, Gina; and The Revellers, again singers. The Songbirds, with The Harmonicas, lined up behind them and fidgeted moving from one foot to the other, as the tension built.

Wendy looked at the competition hopefuls who were left to see what they were up against, *two* singers, Ken Baker and The Tapping Toddlers.

The audience chatted and mumbled including The Songbirds' families as the excitement built.

The compere raised his hands to the audience indicating hush. Taking his cue the audience settled down. "Right," he called as he moved to centre stage. "The clap-o-meter by measuring yours, *you* the audience's applause has brought us to the three remaining contestants. Now the final count for the first, second, and third. Are you ready?"

There was an eruption of cheers and shouts from the audience.

"Okay," he yelled, "here we go." He moved behind the three remaining acts and held his hand up behind Ken Baker. The audience responded with applause, whoops, and shouts. The numbers on the clap-o-meter above the stage lit up the percentage as the numbers climbed. Its counter bounced to 63%, then 68%, and held at 71%.

"That's high," shouted Kay above the dying applause.

There were nods of agreement from the others and a

resounding, *"It's not over till the fat lady sings,"* from Wendy.

Henry standing behind her patted her on the shoulder, smiling. "That's a girl."

Then before The Songbirds knew it the moment of truth had come, the compere moved behind Henry and held up his hand behind him.

The audience went mad, shouting and cheering. The counter jumped to 80% and held . . . then to 83, 87, 90 and back down to eighty-eight with loud sighs from the audience generating more applause and the numbers went up to 91% and held.

The compere quietened the audience, and moved to The Tapping Toddlers lifting his hand to tremendous audience response, applause, shouts, and whoops. The clap-o-meter jumped to 87%, 90, 92, and 94. The Songbirds and The Harmonicas were so moved they joined in clapping, 97% held. "Ladies and Gentlemen," yelled the compere above the applause. "We have a winner."

He led them forward to centre stage. "Ladies and Gentlemen, friends, *The Tapping Toddlers*." The Tapping Toddlers, dancing with excitement, took their bows to an equally excited audience, and the applause continued.

Wendy turned to The Songbirds and The Harmonicas and shouted, "What did I tell you, kids and animals! W.C. Fields was right, you can't beat them."

"Their outfits are lovely," bellowed Emily.

"So are ours!" yelled Kay, with somewhat sour grapes.

Chapter Forty-Three

Paul Weston, dressed in cycling garb, rode his bicycle in and out of the heavy morning traffic as he left London's Hyde Park and made his way into Park Lane. Paul, thirty-five, talked on his mobile phone which was connected to his cycling helmet by Bluetooth technology. "*Dorothy*," he hollered above the sound of the traffic. "*BBC*, Entertainment Tonight, *did you see it over the weekend*? *Yes, this weekend*! *Jane Harris did a piece on a talent show, somewhere in the sticks . . . Some cuties were singing. Get me a copy, I'm five away.*" He bumped up onto the pavement, rode over to the building's entrance and stepped off his Brompton foldup bike. In four swift manoeuvres, he folded the bike up and carried it by the saddle into the building and the elevator.

* * *

On the penthouse floor, the elevator doors opened. Paul and the bike exited passing the gold-lettered sign, reading '*Weston Advertising*'. He took off his helmet as his secretary Dorothy came through the double glass doors to meet him. Dorothy, thirty, auburn-haired and full-figured, was always bubbly and happy. "Morning, Paul."

Paul nodded. "You get it?" Paul, Dorothy and bike headed through the glass doors into the working office. They moved along the hallway past other workers tucked away in the cubical spaces.

"It should have downloaded by now," answered Dorothy as they moved into Paul's penthouse corner office overlooking the London skyline. The dividing wall had a bank of five numbered television monitors, all on with various programmes, but muted.

Paul stood his bike in its module-fitting rack as Dorothy went to the desk and picked up the remote. Paul disappeared into his en-suite bathroom leaving the door open.

Dorothy picked up the phone. "Ian, what monitor are we using?"

Paul came from the bathroom, now wearing suit pants, a shirt plus tie, and his jacket over his arm. He stood in front of the monitors finishing knotting his tie.

Dorothy stood ready with the remote. "Ian's putting it on three," she said as the number three monitor went black. Dorothy fiddled with the remote.

Paul at her side put on his jacket, now an immaculate

City of London businessman. He held his hand out for the remote. Dorothy handed it over. He pressed button after button.

"Nothing!" he snapped tossing the remote on the desk.

Dorothy pressed the intercom on the desk. "Ian?"

Ian's voice came back at them through the intercom. "T'is I."

Paul shook his head. "T'is me the boss . . . No picture here!"

"On my way, *Boss*," yelled Ian.

Paul looked at Dorothy. "Maybe I don't pay him enough," he said with a smile.

Ian, a nerdish-looking young man, for want of a better way to describe him, came through the door. He was in his mid-twenties, glasses, shirt and tie, no jacket. "Morning, Boss."

"Where's the clip, Ian?"

Ian picked up the remote from the desk. "It's here . . . Need to go to input." He hit a button, the screen lit up and Jane Harris was on the screen, backstage at the Bedford Palace.

'*These kids have talent*,' announced the compere. The picture cut to The Tapping Toddlers singing and dancing.

"I watched this," said Ian, "they're very good."

Paul shook his head. "*No . . .* Not them, the others."

"The grannies!" Ian exclaimed.

"Right, the grannies." Paul nodded.

Dorothy looked at Ian and shrugged.

Ian raised an eyebrow. "D told me you wanted the cuties."

"The grannies are cuties," said Paul waiting for the clip to come up.

Ian hit the fast forward to the compere introducing The Songbirds.

The compere was applauding, he finished and was ready for the next introduction. '*Behind that curtain waiting to entertain you are seven ladies. All senior citizens, totalling 454 years between them.*' Applause started up to the chant of, '*Songbirds Songbirds Songbirds.*'

And The Songbirds came on screen.

"Hold it there," said Paul.

Ian froze the picture. Paul got up and went to the door and leaned out and hollered, "*Marty, Pattie,* come look at this."

A moment later Marty, in his early twenties and a little

on the heavy side, and Pattie, the same age, rather pretty, wearing heavy-rimmed black glasses, hurried into the office.

Paul pointed at the monitor. "Think New Age Air Lines, they fly the world campaign. The World Belongs To Me, account. Go, Ian."

Ian hit play and The Songbirds sang as Paul's team watched. They all had one eye on The Songbirds and one on their boss trying to read his thinking and being one step ahead of the game.

Paul waved at Ian. "Stop it . . . Back up."

Ian rewound the clip.

"Hold it," snapped Paul. "Forward a touch."

The Songbirds sang the first line of 'You Belong To Me'.

"Freeze it – Well?" said Paul's arms outstretched.

Ian looked at Paul. "You know they didn't win, right?"

"So! Who cares?" Paul said with a big smile.

Ian looked nonplussed at the others. *Was he missing something*?

Pattie moved to the monitor and studied the frozen frame. After a moment she turned to Paul, her eyes alight with understanding. "Aged, strength, personality, character, *Granny-wise*."

"Got it," he said nodding. "Take the verse, '*Something something silver plane. Jungle all wet in the rain. You're young again. The world belongs to me . . .*' Or something along those lines. I don't know the song!"

"Granny knows best," said Marty, now on Paul's wavelength and inspired.

"New Age Air has been going on about grabbing the seniors' business. Seniors have time on their hands, and money to spend, and New Age Air wants a slice of it," said Paul, starting to pace the room. "These Ladies could be just the ticket. They're fun to watch. Seeing what they do at sixty and seventy, the future is still bright and getting brighter. If they fly New Age Air Lines to see the world, why not all the sixties and seventies and older? They represent the senior market for New Age Air Lines."

"You're right," agreed Marty.

"Let's get on to it," replied Paul the bit between his teeth. "Pattie, find them and sign them. New Age Air Lines is going to love The Songbirds."

Chapter Forty-Four

A full complement of Songbirds with drinks were at their window table at the Chequers, which was busy.

Wendy lifted her glass in a toast. "To Jane Harris, she did us proud."

"She never mentioned the 454-year thing!" murmured Jan.

"She's not as tall as she looks on TV," ventured Dot.

Arlene looked around the table. "Truthfully I was a touch angry we never came first," she admitted.

"Every sixty seconds you spend angry, is a full minute of happiness you'll never get back," remarked Lian.

As one, they turned to Lian, she looked back at them with a frown. "What I say?"

Wendy wrinkled her brow. "You got that out of one of your fortune cookies."

Lian beamed. "Yes, I have more."

"Not now," said Wendy stopping the flow of fortune cookie idioms from Lian's archives.

Kay handed Wendy a pink envelope tied with a red ribbon. Emily giggled softly.

"Ladies, friends," said Wendy getting their attention. "I never had a pretty envelope so Kay did the honours." She turned to Alyson holding the envelope. "This is for you and Tim from us all. We're sorry we didn't get first, but second is better than a kick in the ass, we got £1,500."

"We were first as far as I'm concerned," griped Arlene.

"Ditto," agreed Louise.

"And we'll do more shows," added Lian. "We make money, pay doctor bills."

Wendy handed the envelope to Alyson. With hesitation, she took it as tears rolled down her and The Songbirds' cheeks, tears flowing all around.

Alyson looked at her friends through her tears. "It seems so unfair, you all worked so hard, this should be shared."

"Alyson," said Wendy firmly. "Split between us it would be about £90 each! I don't know about the others, but I do not need £90 that badly."

There was agreement all around, then laughter from all at the table. Alyson rummaged and found a tissue and dried her eyes.

"Are we going to keep singing?" asked Emily.

Wendy pouted. "What at our age!" She smiled. "Give me a vote . . . hands up for yea."

There was a harmoniously unanimous yea, again Alyson's tears ran down her cheeks.

"Thank you all . . . It's such a relief. Tim and I." Alyson stopped mid-sentence seeing Wendy lean forward and look past her into the parking lot.

They all followed Wendy's look, out through the window. A white limousine pulled into a parking space. "Our limo is here, ladies," Wendy said with a laugh.

All were now focused on the limousine, as the chauffeur climbed out and opened the back door.

"Is it a wedding?" asked Dot.

Wendy let out a gasp as she watched her husband Ray step out of the limo, followed by a short dapper man in his fifties, immaculately dressed in a Savile Row suit. "*Ray!*" Wendy sat gobsmacked. "*Ray!*" she exclaimed again. Wendy squeezed onto the window seat between Alyson and Emily all eyes were now on the window with Ray and the dapper man. Ray saw her at the window and waved to her. He and the dapper man headed into the door.

Ray led the man straight over to the ladies, he beamed from ear to ear. "Wendy, ladies, This is Mr Goodman, from London. He's an agent . . . As in theatrical agent," he said, looking at Wendy with a nod and a wink.

Wendy and the ladies sat nonplussed and waited for the plot to unfold.

Johnny showed them a big grin. "Ladies," he said then honed in on Wendy. "Your husband tells me you are the architect of The Songbirds." He reached over and took her hand. "I recognised you all from the *Entertainment Tonight* show." He shook Wendy's hand.

She smiled shyly saying, "I don't know about an architect, but I did bring us all together."

"Then you would, I take it, be the spokesperson for The Songbirds?"

Wendy looked at the others, all riveted waiting for her to reply.

"Spokesperson," she repeated and looked at the ladies. In turn, they nodded in agreement.

Arlene chuckled. "We have a spokesperson."

"Is there someplace we may go to talk about . . ."

Chapter Forty-Five

". . . New Age Air Lines!" said Wendy sitting on the piano stool at home. Ray was perched on the arm of the sofa. They looked at the contract lying on top of the piano in front of Wendy. Johnny stood by the fireplace and was ready to pitch a deal to the boss of The Songbirds.

Wendy shook her head and looked from Ray to Johnny. "You, want to represent The Songbirds to make commercials for New Age Air Lines?"

He nodded and moved over to Wendy and sat on the piano stool next to her. She scooted over a touch to make room. He looked at her, winked and lifted the keyboard lid, and turned to the keyboard.

Wendy looked at Ray who in turn shrugged.

Johnny's hands hovered over the keys for a beat, he then played three introductory chords after which he played and sang an improvised accompaniment to a soliloquy.

'*To be or not to be, that is the question.*
Whether 'tis nobler for The Songbirds.'

He looked at Wendy and exchanged smiles.

'*To introduce New Age Airlines to the world,*

or suffer slings and arrows of a lucrative flourish of

funds into their bank accounts.'

Ray gave out a big smile and a thumbs up.

Johnny continued,

'*The Songbirds Nay*

Take arms against a sea of troubles and shout from

the rooftops

New Age Air Lines is here for the world to benefit

To die, to sleep no more with heartaches of which

airline to travel with

New Age is a fantastic, reliable, and wonderful Airline

supercalifragilisticexpialidocious.'

Ray and Wendy laughed.

Johnny was not over yet,

'*For a time, maybe long, maybe short,*

But it is your sweet wonderful time too, cash in.' he

improvised a fanfare across the keyboard.

Ray and Wendy acknowledged his performance with light applause. He bowed his head.

He spun around on the piano stool and faced her. "What do you say?" he took a pen from his coat pocket, picked up the contract and handed it to her. "What do you say, Wen?"

"I say don't call me Wen."

"Understood," answered Johnny. "Wendy, all the ladies agreed you are the spokesperson, and whatever decision you make, they will abide by and sign on the dotted line."

Wendy looked at the contract in her hands. "It's a big responsibility!"

Johnny nodded in agreement. "It is that, but I'm sure seven senior citizens could make good use of the money," he urged.

Wendy looked over at Ray, who arched both eyebrows.

"I know I wanted you to pack it all in at one-time, sweetheart," said Ray. "But this is not a lifetime job. It would make things a lot easier for Alyson."

Wendy took a deep breath and took the pen from Johnny. "Run it by me once more, please."

Johnny smiled a big smile, he knew he was about to sign The Songbirds. "No problem. You sign with us, World Talent, and I, Johnny Goodman, will represent you for 20% of your earnings. Remember for that I do contracts, paperwork, taxes and I negotiate the best deals for you and the ladies."

Wendy neared the pen to the contract and then had second thoughts. "The commercials will not be degrading in any way toward our age?"

"*No*," said Johnny emphatically.

"That's the last thing we want. We don't want to be put down as being past it, that's the whole point . . . Us staying in the workplace."

Johnny, enthusiasm seeping from his pores, said, "Just the opposite. Weston Advertising wants to play age as strength, personality, and character. Granny knows best. I promise you'll never be looked on as used tea bags."

Wendy looked at Ray. "I've never heard that expression, used tea bags, I think it's even better than chocolate teapots. What do you think, hon?"

"I think it sounds very good and you should climb on board," said Ray.

Johnny gave a nod of agreement to Ray, he knew he was home and dry. "The Songbirds will be seen singing worldwide, from Park Lane to the Golden Gate Bridge, Niagara Falls, Paris, Notre Dame, Arc de Triomphe. Even the Egyptian pyramids. And you are talking a £100,000 cut seven ways. Plus repeats for every block of a thousand showings."

Wendy was inspired by his sales pitch. "I've always liked to travel, see the world split nine ways."

"What?" Johnny frowned.

"We have a seamstress that we could not, and will not, do without and Louise is our stage manager."

Johnny shrugged. "It's your money, so you split nine ways."

Wendy was about to sign but again had a thought. "Okay, I have a request that could be a deal-breaker."

Johnny scowled. "Tell me."

"I want a £10,000 cheque cut for an Alyson Cameron upfront."

"She's one of The Songbirds?"

"Yes."

"Okay, done, less my 20%."

Wendy looked him in the eye. "No. Clean-cut and dry. Ten thousand to the penny, *hers*."

Johnny looked at Ray. Ray raised an eyebrow. Johnny put out his hand. "Deal." Wendy shook his hand, then signed the contract.

Chapter Forty-Six

Johnny Goodman was shown into Paul Weston's office by Dorothy.

Paul looked up from behind his desk, he reached across his desk and offered his hand, and he and Johnny shook hands.

"Any word from the client?" asked Johnny.

Paul leaned back in his chair. "I had a meeting with their concept department and then management, and it went well. New Age is mad about The Songbirds, they want them for the new fly the world campaign."

Johnny gave a thumbs up to Paul. "That's great. I have them signed and sealed. When do we shoot?"

Paul looked at his planner. "Two weeks. Did you get the £10,000 cheque off to this woman Wendy?"

"Done, dusted, and sorted, she should have it by now. I sent it on Monday."

"What was it all about?" asked Paul.

Johnny shrugged. "No idea, but she was ready to let the deal stand or fall by it."

"Right," said Paul. "For whatever reason, I hope it

filled the need . . . We *don't* want any problems along the road."

"There won't be," assured Johnny.

Chapter Forty-Seven

A light flutter of snow fell as Wendy's Smart Car pulled in behind a black transit van parked outside the Cameron house. There were two other cars parked in front of the transit. Wendy climbed out and headed along the garden path to the open front door. Two men in dark suits wheeled out a gurney. Wendy did not have to be told what was being transported on the gurney . . . Under the black blanket was the unmistakable outline of a coffin. She stood aside to let them pass. Wendy recognised the man that accompanied Sue to the door. It was Doctor Grant, he was their doctor as well. Wendy kept her distance while the two talked. After a moment Sue bid him goodbye and then saw Wendy.

Doctor Grant slowed in passing saying, "Wendy, look after them, it's a sad day." As he headed for the gate, Wendy made her way to Sue at the front door, and immediately hugged Sue saying, "I'm so sorry."

Sue stepped back from Wendy's embrace. "He went last night in his sleep. It was peaceful."

"Where's your mum?"

"She's over the worst – she's making tea." With that, she led the way into the house.

* * *

Alyson looked up from preparing tea as Wendy and Sue entered.

"Why didn't you call?" asked Wendy.

Alyson shook her head. "There was no point, you couldn't have done anything bless you."

"I could have been here for you," said Wendy. *Sue was right, what could I have done other than being in the way,* she thought to herself.

"I know, thanks," said Alyson. "I had Sue . . . it was a blessing he went in his sleep." Alyson took a cup from the hook above the countertop and added it to the two on the table and poured tea into each cup. They sat in silence at the kitchen table for a while. Wendy looked at Alyson with concern.

"Alyson, I don't want you worried about this filming thing, you have enough going on. I'll explain to Goodman what has happened and we'll be one short for the filming."

Alyson's head jerked up, her eyes met Wendy's. "*No . . .* you can't do that. Tim would be so angry. *No,* I promised him I wouldn't quit, *whatever*," she said forcefully.

Wendy smiled. "Okay . . . okay, that's fine. I just thought you may need time."

"I have to do as he wanted, I promised," she said, her composure back.

Wendy nodded. "I understand." Wendy took an envelope from her pocket and handed it to Alyson.

Alyson opened the envelope . . . she looked from the cheque in her hand to Wendy and took a breath. "Oh, my God." She handed the cheque to Sue. "Where did you get that?"

"It's the deal I made with Goodman. All The Songbirds agreed."

"Wendy, I'm speechless."

"No you're not, you're talking," she joked.

"Wendy, we don't need this much."

"Well, you have it, like it or not. Buy yourself a hat."

"Somehow I'll pay you all back."

"No, you won't, it's yours. But remember, when we all get our first cheque, you're going to be that much short of yours. It's called an advance." She pointed to the cheque in Alyson's hand. "You've had your's girl."

Chapter Forty-Eight

Snow had covered the ground and hung to the tree branches during the night at St Andrew's Cemetery. If it had not been a cemetery with gravestones everywhere it could have been the backdrop for a Christmas card. Alyson and Sue stood at the head of the open grave, behind them the ground covered by wreaths and flowers. Prayers said and the ceremony over, the Reverend Wilson made his way to the path leading to the gate, ready to offer words of commiseration to friends or family. The mourners followed the reverend's lead and moved away from the grave paying their respects to the widow and daughter in passing. Alyson looked at those remaining at the graveside. The full complement of The Songbirds and husbands, plus Dot, Phil, Louise and Paul. The St. Andrews grave crew hovered out of sight behind a backhoe, ready to attend the closure of Tim's grave. Wendy and Arlene moved around to Alyson followed by the others and in turn hugged her and Sue. Eventually, the small group made their way to Reverend Wilson and said their goodbyes and gave their thanks.

Tim was gone, but not forgotten.

Chapter Forty-Nine

Wendy's Smart Car headlights cut through the light fall of snow, as it came to a stop in the parking lot outside the cemetery gates. A moment later two other car lights shone through the falling snowflakes and stopped. The car lights went out and the car doors opened, out filed The Songbirds, white clouds of warm breath left their mouths and mixed with the cold night air. All were gloved, coated and scarfed for a winter's evening in the snow. They all huddled around Wendy as she took roll call, Arlene, Jan, Kay, Lian, Emily, Alyson and Sue. Dot and Louise were there, although not strictly Songbirds as such, but they were part of the team and helped make The Songbirds The Songbirds.

"Welcome one and all," said Wendy, to murmurs of, *'Its bloody cold . . . I should have worn my long johns.'* Wendy attempted a laugh but they were right . . . it was cold. She went to the gate and lifted the catch, the gate swung open and into St Andrew's Cemetery and in filed The Songbirds.

* * *

In silence, they circled the newly covered grave of Tim Cameron, now covered with his tributes of wreaths and flowers. Teeth chattered, shoulders shivered as The Songbirds linked arms.

"Everyone," said Wendy softly, "we are here because a promise was made . . . thank you all for helping fulfil that promise." She nodded to Alyson.

Alyson softly started to sing, fulfilling her promise to Tim, his favourite song, 'Over The Rainbow'.

The Songbirds joined her in song after the first two lines.

The snow began to fall harder. *'Over The Rainbow', what a crazy song to be singing in a snowstorm*, Wendy thought to herself. But it all made sense as she looked across the tearful faces. *She'd bet her cotton socks that Harold Arlen and Yip Harburg never thought their song 'Over The Rainbow' would go from Hollywood's Oz to Tim Cameron's grave, in a cemetery at Millbrook, England.*

Chapter Fifty

The Songbirds, all smartly dressed in New Age Air Lines cabin crew hostess uniforms, stood exactly three feet apart from each other fifty feet in front of the Arc de Triomphe.

The director's voice called out, *'Do they look centred?'*

From somewhere another anonymous voice yelled, *'Spot on.'*

The director's voice again came to life and yelled, *'Playback.'*

Yet another anonymous voice came from nowhere with a countdown, *'Six, seven, eight'*, and music filled the air and The Songbirds sang.

'Fly the skies in a streamlined plane
See the forests wet with rain
You're among the young again
The world belongs to you.'

Again the director's voice came to life. *'And change.'*

Behind The Songbirds, the Arc de Triomphe disappeared and the background was green for a microsecond. It then became Notre Dame. The Songbirds sang.

'*The world is your oyster*

Go fly with ease

New Age Air Lines flies for you wherever you may please.'

Again the director shouted and behind The Songbirds was a flash of green and they were on the Golden Gate Bridge.

Dot and Louise stood watching with excitement at the side of the giant scaffolding at Pinewood Studios. The scaffolding held the enormous green backdrop that stood behind The Songbirds.

The director shouted, '*Change.*'

In a flash, The Songbirds were in front of the Egyptian Pyramids. Wendy, next to Arlene and somewhat out of breath, muttered, "And you wanted to see the world!"

"Shut up and sing," mumbled Arlene, she too was out of breath.

The director's voice boomed out over the music. "No talking, ladies, sing."

And they did.

'*Fly the skies in a streamlined plane*

See the forests wet with rain

You're among the young again

The world belongs to you.'

The background changed yet again, Niagara Falls, Trafalgar Square, the Statue of Liberty, and so on and so on, eventually coming to an end.

The Statue of Liberty was still on the green backing as the director, a very overweight young man, moved to The Songbirds. "That was very good, ladies, great rehearsal. We'll take a break and do it for real. He moved away leaving them dumbfounded and confused.

"I thought that was for real!" exclaimed Jan.

"I sing for real!" exclaimed Lian.

"God, this is hard work," added Kay.

"It's exhausting," giggled Emily.

Arlene shook her head. "So this is show business?"

"He never said that that was a rehearsal," grumbled Alyson. "I thought that we'd done it."

Louise and Dot arrived with a tray of coffee. "Are we finished?" asked Dot.

"I'm famished," added Louise.

Wendy, after enjoying all the comments, added, "I'll tell you one thing. We did brilliantly. Two appearances and we are the stars of an international, high-flying commercial, forgive the pun."

The Songbirds beamed and exchanged smiles, very pleased with themselves. Lian did little jumps with excitement, then announced, "I do free takeaway for all Songbirds tonight."

They let out a cheer in unison.

"So now we've made it, what do we do next?" asked Jan.

"We can all try plastic surgery," answered Wendy.

All eyes went to her.

"Plastic surgery!" exclaimed Louise gobsmacked. "What do you mean?"

Wendy shrugged. "Cut up our plastic credit cards and laugh all the way to the bank. We're not chocolate teapots anymore."

A voice boomed at them from somewhere, "Right, ladies, ready in ten."

"I really did think we were going to see the world," said Jan.

All agreed in one voice.

Wendy looked at The Songbirds. "You are, but from Pinewood Studios, in good old Iver Heath,

Buckinghamshire UK!"

About the Author

Raymond Austin was born in London and educated at Brighton College. His career began as a stuntman in Hollywood. In the late '60s, he started writing television plays. Brian Clemens, producer and writer of *The Avengers*, promoted him from *The Avengers* stunt coordinator to second unit director of *The Avengers*. Robert S. Baker and Roger Moore then made him the main unit director on an episode of *The Saint*. From then on, he directed episodes for *The Saint* and *The Avengers*. He also worked on other distinguished television shows including *The Prisoner, Black Beauty, The Champions, Jason King, Department S, Alfred Hitchcock Presents* and many other English television shows. In 1970, Austin was named "Outstanding Producer/Director and Writer of the Year" by the London Film Festival for his short film *The Perfumed Garden*. He was nominated for the same award the following year for another short film, *The Sandal*, which also earned him honours at the Cannes Film Festival. In 1972/1973 he was producer/director/writer on *Shirley's World*, the American television show.

Raymond remained in Britain through 1978 and then moved back to the U.S. to work on scores of television shows as a producer, writer and directed 300 hours of TV. By the late '80s, Raymond and his wife, novelist Wendy DeVere-Austin, moved permanently to Fox Haven, their home in the Virginia countryside. Raymond then turned his hand to writing books and in 2001 his first novel *The Eagle Heist, A Beauford Sloan Mystery*, could be found in bookstores worldwide. In 2002 came his second book under the same banner, *Dead Again* and in 2006, *Your Turn To Die*. His first spy thriller, *Find Me A Spy, Catch Me A Traitor*, was released in 2007. After taking a break from writing, Raymond made a comeback with Blossom Spring Publishing and published his *Love Loves A Mystery (Murder all around.) Keep Running Or die* and *Home For The Holiday*. And now *The Chocolate Teapot*.

For more details about Raymond Austin and the shows he has worked on please visit http://raymondaustin.com/

https://en.wikipedia.org/wiki/Ray_Austin_(director)

Other books

By

Raymond Austin and published

through Blossom Spring Publishing

Love Loves A Mystery

Keep Running Or Die

Home For The Holiday

www.blossomspringpublishing.com